Adventures
of
Abby Diamond

Bachelors and Masters degrees in Education, 14 published books through Region 4 Service Center in Houston, Texas and Flaghouse Catalog in New Jersey, Apple Corp Teacher in Mesquite ISD, Author of the Month- Sylvia McGrath's Professor Owl's Newsletter

Adventures of
of
Abby Diamond

BY: Kristie Smith-Armand, M.Ed, TVI

The best and most beautiful things in the world cannot be seen or even touched. They must be felt within the heart.

Helen Keller

iUniverse, Inc.
New York   Bloomington

iUniverse books may be ordered through booksellers or by contacting:

iUniverse
1663 Liberty Drive
Bloomington, IN 47403
www.iuniverse.com
1-800-Authors (1-800-288-4677)

ISBN: 978-1-4401-7013-3 (sc)
ISBN: 978-1-4401-7014-0 (ebook)

Printed in the United States of America

iUniverse rev. date: 10/02/2009

"Out Of SIGHT"
Abby Diamond

By: Jamille Smith
My name is Abby Diamond
My passion is suspense
I can always solve a mystery
That may leave others intense

As I quietly begin to listen
My mind begins to think
And the solution become apparent
As quick as an elephant's wink

Read about my adventures
And I'll take you on a spree
You'll enjoy the thrill and chills
That are all a part of me.

Chapter 1- "Abby Diamond"

Hi. My name is Abby Diamond. I am ten years old and in the fourth grade. I have one older sister, Katy, as well as my mother and father who all live with me. We live in an average-sized two -bedroom apartment in the city.

My dad's name is Jacob. He's so funny, and he makes my sister, Katy, and me laugh all of the time. However, she is acting more like a grown-up and doesn't laugh as much since she is now driving a car. My dad spends his days working in our apartment looking for computer jobs on the Internet and occasionally he finds one.

He is a computer programmer or something like that.

My mother, Caroline, is a fifth grade

teacher at my school. Everyone says that she is so beautiful and that she and I look a lot alike. I do not know what she or anyone else looks like for that matter because I am blind. I have been blind since birth. I cannot see anything except for light and shadows. The doctors told my parents when I was born that I had inherited vision problems that made my eyes not see.

Even though my real last name is Diamond, many of the kids at school think that it is a nickname because my eyes resemble diamonds. People tell me that they are crystal blue just like my mother's eyes and that they look like a sparkling gem.

Being blind is not so bad, though. I have a hilarious vision teacher named Ms. Ashley, who comes to my school every day to help me with my Braille, equipment, and anything else that someone may need.

I also have a wonderful orientation and mobility specialist, O&M for short, named Ms. Harriet.

Ms. Harriet helps me to use my cane correctly so that I can get around places better.

The kids in my class are really cool about my visual impairment except for Jaxson. He makes me so mad. He once yelled and told me to move "my stick" out of his way. I yelled back and screamed,

"It's not a stick, Dummy it's a cane."

One day, he and I are going to come to blows, but enough of old Action Jaxson.

I want to talk about are my two best friends. They are both sighted, so they help me a lot. Their names are Andrea and Neil. Andrea told me that she has dark skin and that Neil has lily -white skin. Andrea's hair color is dark brown and Neils, as I sometimes call her, has bright red curly hair. We are the Three Musketeers.

I have another best friend named Madison who is blind. Madison told me that she was born prematurely which means too early and that she has a condition called Retinopathy of Prematurity, ROP for short. I see Madison at all of the regional events for the blind and have a lot of fun with her. She's a great person, but I still do not have the closeness with her or anyone else like I do with Neils and Andrea.

Our classroom teacher's name is Ms. Adams.

She has such a sweet sounding voice, but she can get tough when she needs to. The other day, old Action Jaxson, tried to get attention by yelling out during our lesson, and Mrs. Adams let him have it. He had to stay after school for detention. I couldn't help but laugh to myself because the old bully got what he deserved.

Another time I was using a piece of equipment that produces Braille called a Perkins Braille Writer.

It makes quite a bit of noise when he said,

"Why don't you go to the school for the blind then I wouldn't have to listen to all of that banging during class."

My third grade teacher marched his behind to the office that day, and Andrea keeps telling me that one day she's going to give him a knuckle sandwich.

Other than the fact that I cannot see, I have had a normal life, nothing too exciting. That's at least what I thought at the time before strange letters written in Braille began appearing, and they were written directly to me.

Chapter 2- "Grand Pop and Nan"

My dad's parents are the coolest. They don't act like typical grandparents. In other words, they travel, laugh and tease with each other all of the time. You would think that they are teenagers. My dad is crazy about his parents and so am I. I know my mom likes my grandparents, but I can see that they get on her nerves sometimes. She works so hard that she sometimes doesn't feel like teasing and laughing with others.

My grandparents never question my dad about why he isn't out finding a job to help out like my mom does. They just come over every weekend and we celebrate whatever there is to celebrate. Grand Pop and I like to walk around the neighborhood. He talks to me about everything that he sees. He always tells me that he will be my eyes. I love it when he describes the colors of the leaves, the trees and whatever else he happens to see that is beautiful.

My grandmother, Nan, is a classical "shop 'til you drop" lady. I think that I have inherited that gene from her. When she and I go shopping, she makes me guide her, count out the money for the sales lady when we make a purchase and try clothes on with little assistance. She and my vision teacher tell me that this will make me an independent adult. "Goody", I think sarcastically.

Nan still takes Katy shopping, too, but Katy only wants to spend time with Brewer. He is her big, bad football -playing boyfriend. Brewer is really nice but I'm not sure if he's playing with all of his marbles, if you get my drift.

One of the things that I like best about being blind is that our school district and regional education centers do a lot of events for the blind and visually impaired. We have a sporting event, shopping trips, technology games, and many other events for the whole family to join in on. My grandparents, parents and sister go to all of my events.

Once I won three first place trophies competing in technology Olympics, and I won first place in using a note taker, operating a Talking Calculator and accessing the Internet. You would have thought that I was Hannah Montana or something by the way everyone in my family and my vision teachers were carrying on.

One time I asked my mom why I didn't know her parents and wondered why they could not be a part of my life. She told me that her dad died when she was really small and that she no longer spoke to her mother whose name is Elizabeth.

"Why don't you speak to her?" I questioned. She only mumbled something like one day when I was older I would understand.

On another day Neil and Andrea were over at my house when they found an old photograph of a woman who looked a lot like me. They told me that she had the same blue eyes and face shape just like mine. My mother politely and coolly told them that that was my Grandmother Elizabeth and then she stomped out of the room. Neil and Andrea made up an excuse and quickly left my house.

So, these are the people who are my best friends and my family. We don't have a lot of money, except for Andrea, but we have a lot of fun.

Chapter 3- "The Bumpy Note"

One beautiful October morning, you know when the air is crisp and chilly and football season is in full bloom, I was walking into the school using a technique with my cane to get to my classroom, when I heard Kylie, a girl in my class say,

"A bumpy letter was left on our classroom door. I bet Abby left it there."

"Left what?" I said to Kylie.

"Here", Kylie said as she gently placed the letter into my hands. "It looks like the bumps that you read and write."

"Hmmm," I thought. It is Braille. I wonder who besides me knows Braille in this school?"

"Thanks, Kylie. I'll decode it and see who brailled the letter because I did not write this."

I began to run my fingers across the few lines of Braille. It simply said,

"Abby, I watch you every day. Please do not tell your parents about this note, it might just kill them."

When you learn Braille, you quickly learn that there are two forms of Braille: grade one and grade two. No, it doesn't have anything to do with grade levels. Grade one Braille is when all of the words are brailled out using the alphabet letters only, and grade two is the more complicated form of reading Braille.

There are over two hundred and forty four contractions when learning to read grade two Braille. Grade two makes the Braille not so long and bulky, so I learned it as quickly as I could.

The reason that I am explaining this is because whoever brailled this note knew the grade two form. For example, they did not Braille out the word y-o-u for you instead they only brailed a y for the word "you" as well as an e for the word "every" and day as a dot 5 "d".

The person who wrote this scary note knew Braille and knew it well.

Chapter 4- "Chill Bumps"

I could not wait until after lunch so that I could meet with Andrea and Neils. My stomach had been so upset after reading the note that I could not eat my lunch. Not that I missed much. I love how the person who writes out the cafeteria lunches describes the luscious whipped mashed potatoes, cream gravy over steak and ripened fruit. It should just read junk that will make you sick and fat.

I first saw Andrea and then had to wait another ten minutes for Neils to show up. For some reason, Neils really gets into the whipped mashed potatoes.

"Let's go over here so no one will see us talking." The three of us walked over behind the building where the rest of the children were playing. We sat down on the porch and I could feel the coolness of the concrete on my legs. I whispered to my friends.

"Why are you being so secretive?" asked Andrea.

"When you listen to what I have to say then you'll know the answer."

"Can anyone see us?" I asked with a shaky voice.

"Girl, are you losing your mind?"

Andrea was getting flustered so I had to talk fast, so I carefully unfolded the note with Braille on it.

"Look what I found on our classroom door. It says that I am being watched every day and that if I tell my parents they might die."

"Oh, no!" screamed Neils. "Let's go to the police now." Neils gets freaked out easily.

"No!" I pleaded. "I am so afraid that something will happen to my family if I say anything to anyone." Andrea voiced that I was correct and that we would think of a plan.

"Don't worry, Abby. The Three Musketeers will stick together. We'll figure this thing out."

My two best friends have a way of calming me down like no other people in the world.

Oh, The Three Musketeers get angry at each other sometimes, but our arguments don't last long. One time after a huge misunderstanding between Neils, Andrea and me, my class took off out of the gymnasium without me. We were all in the second grade at the time. One minute I was sitting and talking to Kylie and then the next minute it was completely quiet. I got so frightened that I screamed bloody murder. Andrea and Neils both ran back into the gym and hugged me until I calmed down.

"What is our next step?" I asked.

Andrea is more of a take-charge kind of person than either Neils or me and she simply said,

"We will wait. We will sit back and wait for the mysterious note-writer to appear and then we'll catch them in the act and turn them over to the police."

I added,

"I knew that I could count on you guys. But as you know, I am blind and can't see, so I will really need the two of you to look out for me and watch for any one who stares at me." Neils laughed at that one.

"A lot of people stare at you, so this is going to be a hard one. For one reason, you're blind and the second reason is that you are beautiful like your mother."

"I wish that I knew what beautiful really meant," I pondered.

"Abby, it's like my mother's perfume that you love to smell. You want to wear it because it is so incredible to smell. You are like the perfume because of your great looks."

"You guys are so great. I feel so lucky to have you as my best friends."

Andrea laughed and said, "Hey. I know how you can make it up to me."

"Please let me know. Just say the word," I said. "Buy me lots of presents for my birthday party."

Andrea burst out into loud bouts of laughter.

"You're funny," I said. "First point is that you're richer than Oprah Winfrey and secondly I am as poor as a church mouse."

We all laughed and walked back inside of the building. My friends had come to my rescue yet again.

Chapter 5- "The Birthday Bash"

"Hurry, Mom! I am going to be late!" I screamed loudly from the bedroom that I share with Katy.

"Okay, you don't need to shout!" she hollered back. I usually don't mind my little small apartment because it can be easy for me to find my way around it pretty quickly but whenever I need my space, like today, I feel so crowded.

Katy stayed in the bathroom primping while she waited on Mr. Brains to pick up and take her to the state fair. They took me last year and we had a great time. I remember smelling all of the wonderful food and hearing a long tall Texan named Big Tex (not a real person) scream out 'hello' in his robotic Texas accent. Katy and Brewer told me that it takes many people to assemble Big Tex each year in October. They also said that he was the size of a two -story building. I ate the most delicious corny dog that I have ever had with yummy gooey mustard. After we ate a funnel cake, French fries, fried cheesecake and a bowl of chili, Katy, Brewer and I rode some ride that made me feel like I was falling backward. I felt sick and well, you don't want to hear the rest of the story.

When I finally made it into the bathroom so that I could comb my hair out, brush my teeth and take care of necessary business if you get my drift, my mom started yelling that we were leaving in five minutes.

"Just a minute," I yelled.

"Oh, Abby. Let me see that comb. Here your long beautiful hair is tangled."

"Ouch, ouch, OUCH!!!" I screamed.

"There your hair looks like it is ready to go to a party. Now I have placed on your bed your jeans with the bling and the purple bling shirt."

"Mom. People don't say bling anymore. Just say the sparkles," I said.

"Okay, we'll let's see. Did you get your

overnight bag, toothbrush, toothpaste, fresh underwear?"

"Mom, gosh you're embarrassing me."

My mom ignored my remark and asked the question again.

"Yes. I am ready to go. Mom, were we able to buy

Andrea anything for her birthday?" I asked softly.

"Oh, yes, Abby. I got her a "bling" shirt just like the one that you are wearing."

We both laughed and she drove me to the party.

When I got to the party, I could hear several kids playing outside. I heard my buddies yell,

"There's Abby. Abby, walk straight, we're over here." Then I felt Neils grab my arm and we ran over to the other kids who were playing. Neils was so excited,

"Abby, I can't wait for our sleep over after Andrea's big party. She's only invited the two of us to sleep over after everyone else has gone."

"Who all is here?" I asked excitedly.

"Almost every one in our class is here except old mean Jaxson and about one hundred cousins."

The party was a huge success. Andrea had a bounce house, a huge blowup slide, a white birthday cake with extra thick white icing. I could smell the delicious vanilla cake. Neils told me that the cake had colorful balloons all over it. She handed me one of the plastic balloons off of the top and I licked off the icing.

Andrea jumped up and down when she opened my present.

"Abby, it's a shirt just like the one you're wearing. Let's get Neils one and they can be our Best Friend shirts."

All afternoon we bounced in the bounce house, went up and down the slide and watched or in my case, listened to a magician do magic tricks. He was great and used hand-over-hand, in other words, he guided my hands with his and helped me to do some of the tricks. The kids all yelled and clapped for me.

Everything was going great until Andrea's mother came up to me and asked if my father or grandfather had stayed for the party.

"No," I answered, "My mom brought me and then dropped me off."

"Oh," Mrs. Williams said. "Some man was following you around when you were jumping in the bounce house. He also watched you when you were with the magician. He must have seen me watching him because whenever I walked towards him to ask him who he was, he just disappeared quickly. It was almost as if he disappeared into thin air."

Andrea and Neils both heard Andrea's mother and came over to me.

"We have got to be careful and get behind what's going on around here," said Andrea.

"Don't worry, Abby, we won't let you down."

"I know. You guys are great and I won't let some stranger ruin my day. If someone comes near me, I'll do this and this." I began demonstrating how I could use my cane as a dangerous weapon.

"Please don't tell Ms. Harriet on me. She said that the cane is not a toy and should only be used for safety reasons."

That night after Andrea, Neils and I changed into our pajamas; we went down the stairs in search of more delicious birthday cake.

"I had the best birthday ever," said Andrea. "I love my new purple bike, my rollerblades and my new ipod, but the best gift is having my best friends spend the night." We were all laughing in the kitchen and eating more cake when we heard a noise. It was the back doorknob on the screen door slowly turning.

Chapter 6- "More Bumps"

We all screamed. I guess that Neils and Andrea got so scared that they ran off and left me standing alone in the kitchen. I grabbed my cane so that I find my way back to the staircase, but because I was in a panic, I dropped my cane. I fell on the ground and began screaming loudly. Mr. and Mrs. Williams came running down the staircase towards me while Andrea and Neils were closely behind them.

"It's going to be alright," said Mr. Williams' comforting voice. I held onto his large arms tightly.

After we had all calmed down and after Mr. Williams checked around their new large house, Andrea's parents went back to bed and told us to stay inside and to call them if we heard anything else. Andrea and I were talking about how scary the sound of the door was when we noticed that Neils was missing.

"Neils, where are you?" we screamed. 'Adventurous Neils' had actually gone outside and found a note taped on the outside of the door.

Neils yelled, "Look what I found. It's another bumpy note written in Braille. Abby, what does it say?" After Neils carefully placed it in my hands, I tried to steady my shaky fingers to read the note.

The note read, "Abby, I watched you enjoy yourself all day and that makes me very happy. I am sorry to frighten you. I just want to be near you and your family."

"That's it," screamed Neils. "I am going to the police."

"Now, wait a minute," Andrea said sternly. "We still have to catch this person red handed."

"He has a red hand?" I asked.

"Hahaha" squealed Andrea and Neils. "No, it means that we have to catch this person with the note in his or her hands and then tell on them. "

"The second note doesn't really sound that

scary to me. But for some reason, they can't let you know who they are," said Andrea.

"You don't think that old Jaxson could be behind this, do you?" asked Neils.

"If he is, I'll take 'my stick' as he calls it and do this and this and this." I took my cane and began demonstrating all over again how I could use it as a dangerous weapon. This time Neils and Andrea started playing along.

"Aaaagh, you got me!" screamed Neils.

"Ouch, ouch, ouch," screamed Andrea. We all began to laugh and have fun again.

That night we spread out our sleeping bags and they watched while I listened to some of our favorite movies. We also more of Andrea's delicious birthday cake.

Chapter 7- "Ms. Ashley's Call"

Monday morning was a bummer after having so much fun all weekend at Andrea's house. I took out my note taker, turned it on while putting on my headphones so that I wouldn't disturb that creep Jaxson and began doing boring Language Arts. Ms. Ashley finally came and took me out of this prison.

"Where have you been?" I asked. "Ms. Adams was going on and on about subject verb agreement so much that I was ready to scream. Man!" I complained.

"Well, hello to you, too, Abby," Ms. Ashley chuckled. We walked to what I refer to as the Braille room.

In reality it is an old used bookroom, but Ms. Ashley and I love it and call it our secret hideaway. We Braille, print and work on the internet in our little palace.

She also makes me use the phone to call and ask questions to places of business. For example, one time I called a pizza place to ask what time they opened. We do little things like this because they will make a big difference in me being independent and relying on others for information. My parents told me one day that Ms. Ashley is one of the best teachers around.

"Today we're going to make sure that you are using your spell check correctly on your note taker. Is your printer still printing out correctly so that all of your teachers can see in print what you are brailling?"

"Yes, and they love that they don't have to figure out the Braille," I replied.

"We wouldn't do that to them," Ms. Ashley stated. Ms. Ashley sounds really young. I bet that she isn't much older than Katy and Brewer. She once told me that her hair was the color of chocolate and that she had chocolate covered eyes and caramel colored skin. "Yummy," I said when I was in kindergarten.

She laughs all of the time because she thinks that I am hilarious. However, like Ms.

Adams, she can get tough when she wants. She once told me to stop blaming my note taker for the reason that I was not turning in my work. I told her that it was broken, but that didn't fly with her.

She said, "Why can't you use your Brailler then?" She had me on that one. Ms. Ashley never lets me get away with anything. "No excuses" is her motto. Mine is 'Born to shop but forced to work'. Actually that one belongs to my Nana.

After Ms. Ashley checked my note taker and finally complimented me on how I was using it, the phone rang inside of our little office that we use. It was Ms. Ashley's doctor.

"Abby, do you mind if I take this call down the hall in the Teachers' Lounge? It is pretty personal."

"Not at all," I said. "Just don't send me back to class too early." Ms. Ashley got up from her chair and went down the hallway. I could hear her heels making a clomping sound that began to fade as she got further away from me.

When I knew she was gone, I pulled out my headphones and began listening to one of my favorite songs. Ms. Ashley lets me do that at times on Fridays after we have worked hard all week. I was enjoying the song, when I heard footsteps coming up behind me. Actually, I heard footsteps coming from two different people.

"Who's there?" I asked in a shaky voice. No one spoke.

"Who's there?" I asked again only louder this time. No one spoke again. I felt my heart drop to the bottom of my chest. I got hot and cold at the same time.

I panicked and began to yell, "Help me!"

Chapter 8- "Action Jaxson to the Rescue"

"Please God, help me", I said quietly. What could I do? I just sat still and began to tremble when out of the blue I heard smaller footsteps come running down the hall.

"I'll save you!" screamed Jaxson. "Are you okay, Abby?" "Hey, who are you two?" I heard adult voices, one man and one woman, beg him to keep his voice down.

Jaxson screamed, "Get out of here!"

Next thing I knew he grabbed our custodian, Old Man Massey's broom and began swatting at the two intruders. I could hear loud adult footsteps running away.

I heard the man's voice say, "That kid is crazy. Let's leave before he causes a bigger scene. Here grab my arm."

Jaxson knelt beside me. "Are you okay, Abby?" he added softly.

"Yes Jaxson. Thank you so much. I don't know what would have happened if you had not come. Who were those people and what did they look like?" I asked.

"Well, it is hard to say because the woman was wearing a hood over her face and the man had a scarf wrapped around his neck, but the woman looked a little like, well, looked a lot like, your mother, only older."

I had to take all of this in for myself to process. Like my mother but only older? That just didn't make sense to me. My mother's classroom was two –hallways away from me, and the only man that she ever even talked to besides my dad was Old Man Massey, our custodian.

She talks to him because he cleans her boards and keeps her classroom looking nice. Mom gets mad when we call him Old Man Massey. She would really be mad if she knew the song that we made up about him.

"Old man Massey, his breath is really gassy." We crack ourselves up over that one. I feel kind of bad, though, when we sing that song because when I am waiting in my mom's classroom after school, he gives me candy. I think that he feels bad for me because I am blind, so I let him.

Ms. Ashley doesn't like it when I let people feel sorry for me because of my visual impairment and allow them to give me special privileges, but what's a girl going to do? I have been given extra chicken nuggets in the classroom and all of the teachers say hello to me daily. One time Neils told me to show an old man my cane so that he would give us free cotton candy at the fair. Too bad her plan failed. He just said in a grouchy voice, "That will be fifty cents, hurry up and pay and move on."

Anyway at the end of the day, I asked my mom if she came into the Braille room as I call it.

"No, Abby," she said. "I don't have time to run to the restroom with thirty fifth graders around me all day." Mom sounded tired, so I did not push the issue. Later that night, my mom's voice didn't sound so tired when my dad announced at the dinner table that he not only got a new job today, it was a job making more money than he had ever dreamed of.

The job came through an advertisement on the Internet right to his email. It was for a computer whiz, like my dad, to come and work at this huge and well-respected company. Dad told us that he went on the interview without anyone knowing because he was afraid that he would let us down again. That last word hit me hard in the stomach. Whether my dad has money or not, he has never let me down for one second.

My mom's voice sounded so excited. She sounded like a girl Katy's age.

"Oh, Jacob," she screamed. "I am so proud of you." There was still more good news to come.

"With my new job and big raise, we are going to buy a large home, so that our girls can not only have their own bedrooms but bathrooms as well. Oh, yes and a swimming pool will be added."

We were all screaming and clapping loudly when my cell phone rang. It was Neils speaking loudly, even louder than usual.

"Abby, you are not going to believe this. But the Braille note person left me a message in print on my door. It says for me to bring you, Andrea, Katy and Brewer to The Burger House at noon on Saturday where we will find a hidden treasure. What do you think we should do?" I told Neils that I would call her back after I told her about my dad's new job and our new house.

"I'll think on this one. Let's talk to Andrea and see what she thinks tomorrow at school."

After I hung up the phone with Andrea, I was so excited that I could barely sleep, and my mom must have felt the same way because I could hear her laughing loudly for the first time in a year.

Chapter 9- "The Scavenger Hunt"

The next morning my mom made all of us blueberry pancakes from scratch. I smelled the sweet aroma as soon as I woke up. Have you ever had a wonderful moment when everything seems to be going your way for once? That's the way this morning was. It was early October and the crisp air was really getting chilly. I grabbed my cane and put on my red wool jacket and headed out the door. I always met Neils at the bottom of our steps.

"Good morning," she screamed.

"Hey, Neils. I cannot wait to tell Andrea about your note. What kind of treasure do you think it is?"

"Maybe money?" questioned Neils. "Abby,

I'm glad about your new house, but I am going to miss walking to school with you everyday."

"I know," I said, "but me living further away means that you'll have to spend the night more."

When Neils and I saw Andrea and told her about the printed note, she was freaked out.

"I do not like the sound of this. Why do these quacks want Katy and Brewer to come along? Why would two adults want to follow around children? They must be creeps or really strange." Andrea replied.

The bell rang so we all went into the classroom. Jaxson came up behind me and actually said hello to me. I smiled and said hello back. After all, he did save my life.

Ms. Adams was up at the board going on and on about key words to solve math problems for another dumb test that all of us had to take when I completely fell asleep. I began dreaming and it was just terrible. An old woman wearing a hood was grabbing me by the hair and an old man was holding my mother around the neck.

"Let her go!" I screamed. The next thing I heard was laughter. The class was laughing at something and so was Ms. Adams. They were laughing at me.

"Am I keeping you awake, Abby Diamond?" Ms. Adams asked.

"Oh, I'm sorry. I didn't get much sleep last night." At the end of the day when Neils and I were walking home, Brewer and Katy pulled up in his red mustang.

"What's going on Abster?" Brewer chuckled.

"Oh, hi Brewer. Hi Katy. I have something that I want to talk to you two about."

Katy was scared after hearing all of the details of the brailled and printed notes. Brewer wanted to call some of the members of the football team and scare the living daylights out of the ones who were leaving the note, but Katy had a plan.

"Let's go along with what the note asked us to do. We will all stick together. Brewer, you can ask T-Bone to come along too just for more protection."

T-Bone was six foot six inches tall and bigger than Shaquille O'Neal. He played center on Brewer and Katy's high school football team.

Katy continued, "We'll have everyone meet at The Burger House tomorrow morning and maybe we can discover who is behind this madness."

The next day we all met at The Burger House at exactly noon. Brewer and T-Bone ate three hamburgers each while we waited for something to happen. Then we waited some more. About one o'clock we were about to call it a day when a kid about Katy's age who worked at The Burger House came up to our table.

"Hey. Some lady just gave me a hundred dollar bill and told me to hand Abby these four envelopes. It was creepy. She was hanging on to some old guy and kept hiding her face." I reached my hands out in front of me for the boy to hand me the envelopes.

"Can she talk?" he asked stupidly.

"Boy, can she ever," chuckled Andrea.

"Just hand me the notes," I said starting to get ticked off at everyone.

The first envelope simply said to drive to Ivy Street and to look for the four sisters. 'One sister is smaller than the other three'. Look around her and you'll find the next clue to the treasure.

We all jumped into T-Bone's SUV and took off to Ivy Street.

"Where do the four sisters live?" Katy wondered aloud.

"I think I know," replied Brewer. "I know because I know every girl that lives on this street."

"Oh, please," Katy's voice sounded disgusted.

"I really know," screamed Andrea. "Look across the street from the white house. See the identical four trees that are standing in a line? The one on the end is slightly smaller than the other three." Andrea is not only smart, she's really smart and she was exactly correct.

Sitting to the left of the smaller tree was a red box tied with a blue bow. Inside of it were four tickets to see Hannah Montana and two tickets for the Dallas Cowboy game that same weekend.

"Wow! Can T-Bone and I have the Cowboy tickets?" Mr. Brains wanted to know.

"No, I think that Abby would much rather go to a Cowboy game than to see Hannah Montana," Neils added sarcastically. We all laughed so hard. Life was getting good. Too good really! What was going to happen to change all of this?

The next envelope said in Braille to drive

to the football stadium and find the place where Brewer won Katy's heart.

"Gross," I screamed.

"I can lead everyone now," Katy beamed. It was my first high school football game. Brewer started to throw a pass to the receiver but the receiver was being covered, so he ran the play in himself and scored the final touchdown. I was standing in the stands, when he ran over and screamed up at me, 'Hello!... will you go out with me tonight?"

Katy's voice sounded too sweet like when you eat too much syrup or something. The encounter between Katy and Brewer was in the community newspaper the next day after the winning touchdown. My mother told it showed Katy looking down and smiling at Brewer and he was looking up at her with his arms reaching up towards her. I'm too young to care about that kind of icky romance stuff.

We walked out on the football field and right behind the goal line was another red box tied with gold bow, school colors. Inside of it had my and Katy's name on two gift certificates for the mall. They were each worth one hundred dollars each.

Underneath the box written in Braille it said,

"Buy yourself something nice to wear to the concert." I could not believe what was happening. Who had come into our lives and made everything so much better?

We all jumped back into the SUV and everyone waited anxiously for me to read the third envelope. It simply said,

"Our Lady knows that being blind is a hard obstacle to overcome but travel to this one place in town weekly for your daily strength."

"It has to be my church," added T-Bone. "It's one of the largest churches in town. It's called Our Lady of the Hills." T-Bone drove us quickly to the other side of town and sure enough waiting for us on the steps of T-Bone's church was another red box with a white bow. Inside of the box was another one hundred dollar bill. On the bill was a printed note that said,

"Have lunch on us." The boys were hooting and hollering when I told them to be quiet.

"Guys, things are too good to be true. Why is someone being so nice to a bunch of kids?" I worried.

"Because we're so cute and popular," laughed Katy.

We all decided to eat at a trendy and typically expensive steak restaurant across town called Kristie's.

After we were seated I began to hear just how much football players can eat. It was a great restaurant. We all crowded in a high booth and ate an appetizer, a meal and a hot apple pie with vanilla ice cream on top. The food was incredible. The waitress even asked me if I wanted my menu in Braille. Finally, we opened the last envelope. It only said,

"Tell your mother that I love her." My heart dropped. Did my mother have a stalker?

Chapter 10- "Aunt Dana"

Who made up the tradition of having yearly family reunions? I never admitted to my sweet father how much I hated going to his family reunions. I know that my mother and I share the same opinion about the Diamond family reunions but we never say it aloud.

Oh, I think that my dad, my Grand Pop and Nan are the greatest but add one sour person with no social skills to the mix and you have yourself an afternoon of dread.

That one person in my dad's family is my Aunt Dana. She thinks she's all of that with two snaps and a twist according to my mother. In other words, she's arrogant, rude and a snob.

Not that Dana has anything to be snoddy about. She works hard like everyone else, has a whiny voice and complains all of the time about not having found Mr. Right. I want to tell her to stop whining, shut up sometime and maybe, just maybe someone will show up for her to nag and make miserable. My dad loves his sister, so he tries to cover up for her rudeness by constantly saying that she doesn't mean to come across the way that she does. My mother usually responds with a "whatever" remark.

Another thing about Aunt Dana that drives my mother and me crazy is that Aunt Dana asks about me to another person when I am sitting right there. For instance, last year she asked mom how I was doing.

My mother said, "Dana, Abby is right here. Why don't you ask her yourself?" Then she talked to me like I was in the first grade.

"Hi Abby. How are you? Is school fun for you?"

"Oh, yes. A blast," I tell her.

She doesn't pick up on my sarcasm because she thinks that I have other special needs just because I can't see. She still buys me toys for first graders or books on tape that a kindergarten child would enjoy.

So, here we were again Mom, Aunt Dana and me sitting on my grandparents living room couch waiting on the food to be ready. I could hear adults yaking, my little cousins running around and playing, and worst of all Aunt Dana whining about men again.

She has always preferred Katy over me because Katy looks like Aunt Dana and my dad. 'Katy this and Katy that'. She began talking to my mom about how beautiful Katy was and that she has a picture of herself as a teenager that looked just like Katy. What is really funny is that Katy doesn't care for Aunt Dana anymore than I do. Katy spoke to Aunt Dana and quickly went outside to play with the younger cousins. I could have played outside too but I felt the need to rescue my mother and not to leave her stranded beside Ms. Obnoxious.

"I hope that Katy doesn't let men treat her wrongly like I have," moaned Aunt Dana.

"Oh, neither she nor Abby will put up with anything but the best," my mother retorted.

"Oh, does Abby have a little boyfriend," she asked stupidly.

"Not yet," I replied. "But the next blind dumb boy that I meet is mine." It got really quiet. My mother said, "Abby, watch your manners."

Aunt Dana replied, "Abby, I didn't mean to hurt your feelings. Would you like for me to get your food for you. It's ready."

"Sure," I said. "I would love for you to fix my plate, bring me a napkin and silverware and chop up my meat for me." My mother spoke up.

"Abby, go get your plate yourself and apologize to Dana."

"I'm sorry," I said under my muttered breath. Aunt Dana finally moved on to other victims. I could hear her say, "That's my impaired niece. Poor little thing. I don't know why they don't send her off to the school for the blind. She could meet a lot of nice blind kids."

Even though my dad takes up for his kid sister, my Grand Pop and Nan make disgusted noises about their daughter. They say stuff like "maybe one day she'll grow up and get over herself."

After the torturous afternoon we got to go and see my favorite aunt. It's my mother's sister, Aunt Blake. She is the coolest of all cool. She doesn't treat me any differently than she does anyone else. She's funny and laughs all of the time. When I am with her, I have the best time. Aunt Blake buys me age appropriate things, too, like cool music and great clothes. My mother has told me that she is beautiful. Mom said that she has long blonde hair like mine, blue eyes and a full mouth with beautiful white teeth.

Aunt Blake takes me shopping, skating and once took me on a vacation just the two of us to Fort Lauderdale. We swam in the ocean, ate the whole week and shopped at the entire gift shops along the coast. She has the shopping gene, too I guess.

My aunt Blake is an artist and a great one at that. She actually makes a great living for a company doing their art design. She also paints during her recreational time and sells her paintings for the big bucks. She encourages me to keep writing. I enjoy making up stories and keeping them in my note taker. She told me that maybe one day, I could be a novelist. I think that I will write a novel about a stupid aunt named Dana that thinks her blind niece is dumb. I guess I'll have to change the names to protect the prejudice and ignorant.

When we got home from our day with the relatives, Katy thought that I had left my Braille pages on the porch.

"Here are Braille papers, pick them up

yourself next time, Missy." I felt of the papers and knew immediately that I had not left Braille papers on my porch. Number one reason is that I don't use standard Braille paper much anymore because I have my note taker and emboss the work on a different type of paper. The number two reason is that when I do use that type of Braille paper on my Braille writer it's only in math class at the school.

I slid my fingers over the Braille. It read,

"Don't let anyone make you feel bad about yourself. We all have some type of disability whether it's physical or emotional. Guess which one your aunt has?" My heart began to beat rapidly. Besides members of my family, who else knew about Aunt Dana and her socially challenging disability? I also shuddered because whoever was leaving the notes was once again following my family and me.

Chapter 11- "The Concert"

The next week, Katy and mom took me shopping for a new outfit. Katy and I made up some lie about one of Katy's friends getting her tickets. Katy also misled my mother by saying that she had saved up enough money to buy the two of us outfits for the concert.

I bought a beautiful soft purple sweater with a new pair of jeans. I also had enough money to buy new earrings that matched my sweater and a pair of brown leather boots. I bought a new leather brown purse that matched my boots.

Katy and I had such a great time together like we use to before she turned sixteen and began dating Mr. America. I know that Katy has sometimes been pushed back because of my disability. She doesn't want to be resentful but I know at times it really is hard on her and the rest of my family.

That night of the concert was the best ever. Katy drove us in Mom's old rusty burgundy Four Runner. When we got to the concert the parking was awful. I could hear the crowd and cars honking, but that didn't stop what was to be one of the best nights of my life.

Neils and Andrea described for me what they were wearing after they told me how much liked my outfit. Neils was wearing a blue jean skirt with a turquoise colored jacket with sparkles that I could feel and a simple white cotton shirt. She also was wearing a new pair of brown boots. Katy and Andrea both commented on how cute she looked. Andrea who is the stylish one by far was wearing a pair of black jeans with a white jacket that had big black buttons and a white sash. She was wearing a sparkled black tank top underneath her white jacket and was wearing new black boots. Katy told me that her hair was pulled up in a high ponytail so that you could see her black hoop earrings.

Hannah Montana was incredible. We all sang, danced and had the best time ever. Mom gave me enough money so that I could buy a CD and t-shirt with Hannah's picture on it. Andrea, Katy and Neils all took turns describing what Hannah was wearing during each costume change, what the stage looked like and what was going on around us.

It was the best time ever.

Chapter 12- "The Big Breakup"

The next morning after the concert all of the excitement stopped. Mom and Dad began looking for houses, Dad was gone all of the time and Mom's voice began to sound tired again.

We met Dad's new boss one evening. His name was Mr. St. Claire. He was the nicest man and mom said that he had more money than God. I know then it must be incredibly rich because Mr. St. Claire brought Katy and me both presents the night that dad brought him home. He gave Katy a silver bracelet and me a necklace that had my initials written in Braille.

Something else really strange began to happen. The notes just stopped coming. All of the excitement just stopped, just like that. Even though I had been freaked out by the notes and the sudden appearance of the stalkers at school that day, I have to admit that the events gave me something to look forward to.

The big news around our house and the high school was that Katy and Brewer broke up. Katy was so unhappy. She stayed on the couch and started eating potato chips all of the time. I felt sorry for her even though I always knew that she could do better than Mr. Brainless.

One day when Katy was lying around and moping, our mother came stomping into the living room and boy was she mad.

"Why didn't you two tell me that someone has been leaving you notes in Braille? I bumped into Mrs. Williams in the grocery store and she was still terribly worried about you, Abby. Why didn't you tell me? I am going to the police and show that stalker that he or she cannot come near my family again. Whether it's sympathy or weirdness I will not tolerate this type of behavior from adults or children as far as that goes. You two girls will let me know from now on if anyone and I mean anyone approaches you or offers you anything. Is that understood?" Mom screamed.

"Yes," we both said in unison.

"Good then we are clear. You two will not use the phone either the land phone or the cell phone or the computer all weekend. Your dad and I have to close on our new home and while we are doing that both of you will clean this nasty apartment and box up and label all of your items." She then stomped out of the apartment and slammed the door hard.

My mother is usually a reasonable adult and not hot headed at all, so I knew just how upset she really was.

The next weekend was the worst ever. It rained, Katy cried and I was tired of boxing up all of my junk. I used my Braille label maker to mark all of my boxes. Some of the items I felt of but simply forgot what they were so I labeled them "things I forgot about" because I wasn't about to ask Ms. Crybaby anything.

I finally got sick of listening to her squabble, so I shouted,

"Katy, get over it. He is as dumb as dirt and he stinks underneath his armpits." The room got really quiet. I just sat still. Then out of nowhere I heard Katy burst out laughing.

She was laughing so hard that she could barely breathe. I started laughing, too. She grabbed and hugged me and then I knew that she was going to be fine.

Chapter 13- "Boo"

I know that I am growing up really fast and that this will probably be the last time that Neils, Andrea and I can get away with going Trick-or-Treating without grownups telling us that we are too old and that the candy is only for the little ones. This year Mr. and Mrs. Williams are taking us around to some haunted houses and Trick-or-Treating in their, oops, I now mean our neighborhood.

Neils, Andrea and I kept discussing what kind of costumes that we would be wearing for Halloween one day while we were eating my mother's homemade chocolate chip cookies. I love to eat them with they are fresh out of the oven, all warm and gooey.

"Let's go as The Three Blind Mice," I said laughing.

"Not funny, Abby," my mother barked.

"Okay, okay. What about the three of us going as The Three Omigos or The Three Musketeers?" I asked.

"We already did the Musketeers," said Neils.

"Why don't we all go as something different from each other since this is our last year," Andrea stated. We all agreed and sat in silence trying to come up with individual ideas.

"I have the greatest idea," Neils beamed. "But first I have to talk to your mother, Abby."

"Great, but I still can't think of what I want to be," I fretted. After several minutes my mind started clicking on a few unusual ideas. The three of us decided not to tell each other what we were going to be and would surprise each other on October 31st.

Finally, Halloween day arrived. Both of my best friends and I would meet in front of the Williams' large home, We would Trick-or-Treat for a while and then go to the haunted houses out in the country.

Mom helped me to dress as one of my favorite characters from a novel that we read in the fourth grade named <u>Doll House</u>

<u>Murders</u> by Betty Wren Wright. I was going as the old grandpa. I wore my dad's working overalls. I also put on an old red and yellow plaid shirt that Dad paints in and a straw farmer's hat. My painted side burns and a beard on my face. My cane would be appropriate because I was going as an old man.

When Andrea and Neils saw me they began to rip roar laughing and so did Mr. and Mrs. Williams. My mother was laughing equally as hard but not at me but at Neils. Neils, had borrowed one of my old canes, and high contrast glasses and was dressed like Helen Keller.

Andrea was cutely dressed as a black cat. Mom said that she had sparkles all across her eyelids, a black body suite with a tail and a cute short red skirt.

After we went from house-to-house grabbing the goods, it was time to go to the haunted houses on Grubb Road. The first house we went to was fun but not scary at all. We walked through the house and a few scary monsters yelled at us and told us to put our hands in some spaghetti and grapes while trying to make us believe that they were guts or something like that. Neils screamed her head off but just to make Andrea and me laugh.

However, the next haunted house scared the day lights out of us. Mr. and Mrs. Williams politely told the teenagers working there that one of the children in the group was blind. Without asking they assumed the blind kid was Neils, so they carefully took Neils by the hand and quickly led her to safety. Neils never told them any differently because they were so nice to her and gave her a small and decorated bag of candy.

Now, the real blind girl, me and Andrea were going through all kinds of torture. Kids were grabbing and pulling on us, throwing silly string and all kinds of junk at us. Then I heard a chain saw. I really freaked out over this one. I screamed so loud that Mr. Williams broke through the teenage barrier at the front door and ran straight to Andrea and me. He led us out, we found Neils and left. Mr. and Mrs. Williams are the greatest. They didn't want us to go home after that terrifying house, so they took us to their church where there was a carnival and a really neat hayride. The hay itched but I don't think that I have ever had so much fun.

That night I ate too many candy bars and threw up.

Chapter 14- "Moving Day"

No one wants a blind kid around when they are trying to move. I kept getting pushed this way and that way. At first my family would say, "excuse me" or "watch out" then it was "get out of the way" or "why don't you go play with the computer". I told my family that I was being discriminated against because I was blind.

"Is that so?" my mother said.

"Yes," I stated with an attitude.

"Well, I don't want you to feel that way, so why don't you put your cane down and start taking all of your boxes to the moving van, Ms. Feel-Sorry-For-Herself." Me and my big mouth. My family and vision teachers never let me pull the sympathy card. Darn them. If I'm every truly frustrated or depressed about being visually impaired they are all so great and help me to overcome the feelings but they all know when I'm trying to pull one over on them.

I loaded more boxes than I ever knew that I had. I kept feeling for the Braille to make sure that they were my boxes and that someone wasn't pushing their boxes off on me. Moving Day wasn't as much fun as I thought that it would be. Everyone was at each other's throats. Dad started trying to boss every one around, Mom was a big grouch and Katy was back to moping around and acting like a teenager again. Katy and I had not seen the new house, so we didn't know what to expect. It was actually located near Andrea's house.

When we pulled up in our new driveway everyone's attitude changed. Katy told me that the new house was huge and that it had a beautiful lawn and gardens everywhere. We jumped out of the car and she led me around using a sighted guide technique. Sighted Guide is when I don't use my cane. I take hold of the person's arm and they lead me around. Our family walked into the new house and began walking around.

"Girls, this is a new house to us, but it has

been in my family for hundreds of years," Mom said.

The house had two stories, a huge built-in blue swimming pool, a room that was made into a workout room, four bedrooms, four and a half baths, an enormous living room area, a kitchen five times as big as the one in the apartment and three fireplaces. Katy took my arm and spoke, "I'm so glad that you get your own room. Let's go and see what it is like. Have you seen the television show where a group of experts go out and build a new home for people who have needs? I felt just that lucky.

My new room was painted my favorite color, purple. It had a huge canopy bed, a desk with all of my Braille technology like my printer and embosser and a new television with a DVD player that hung from the wall. My bathroom was painted shades of periwinkle blue and purple. Katy said it was beautiful.

Katy's bedroom was painted with her favorite colors: mauve, green and a cream color. She told me that her bathroom was done in the same colors as my bedroom.

We went outside and turned on the Jacuzzi since it was too cold to go swimming. Thanksgiving was next week, so the Jacuzzi was just what we needed.

After Dad cooked out on his new built-in grill, we ate grilled hamburgers, chips and drank sweet ice tea, yes even in the winter, Texans drink ice tea. We took a dip in the new Jacuzzi and when bubbles came out they came out in strong currents but it felt great. I was getting a little warm but felt too good to get out.

The first night that I spent in my new bedroom all by myself was the best night ever. I shut the door, turned on my ipod and felt happier than I had felt in a long time.

It was the middle of the night; I felt a hand touch my arm. I jumped up to see who it was.

"Mom, please let this be you," I begged.

"No, it isn't your mother. Don't say a word and come with me." I felt something sharp and pointy like long fingernails scrap my arm. The person grabbed me and then pulled me up and started making me walk towards the door, and I could smell a foul odor coming from whoever this was.

"No," I screamed and then I woke up. I felt around in the darkness and it was very quiet. It was another nightmare, but least this time I wasn't waking up to the laughter of my classmates.

Chapter 15- "The Thanksgiving Program"

It was just my luck. Our grade level would put on the annual Thanksgiving program at our school. Why do people think that the blind kid has to be the center of attention? It isn't like we don't get attention most of the time anyway. We were suppose to sing a song about being thankful or something like that and then Neils and I would walk out together arm-in-arm together and introduce the cast of The First Thanksgiving. Isn't that an original and creative title?

Poor old Jaxson was assigned the role of the turkey. I think that was after he asked Ms. Adams why she cut her hair so short and then the big mouth added that she looked like his Uncle Frank.

We practiced after school every day for a whole week. During one class one day, I showed Andrea and Neils how to make a turkey on the Braille writer.

"That is really cool," Andrea gleamed. "I'll show you how to make another kind of turkey." She took my hand and traced around it with Tulip paint. After Tulip paint dries, it makes a tactual drawing. I could feel the shape of the turkey feathers that were drawn in paint.

The night of the program, my parents, Nan and Grand Pop, and Katy all piled into my mom's brand new SUV. Since Dad has been working at his new job and liking it so well, he has been even more generous than usual and bought himself, and mom new cars. I got a cell phone, ipod and a new note taker and Katy squealed with excitement when she got her very own laptop with a great setup.

On the way to the program, I heard Dad ask Mom if it was okay to invite his boss, Mr. St. Claire and his wife over for dinner before Thanksgiving. My mom was fine with that, so we would get to meet the boss' misses soon. Joy, I thought.

After we did the Thanksgiving program, all of the kids and parents were standing around and talking. I heard Jaxson's voice in my ear. I could feel his turkey feathers sticking into my ribs.

"Ouch, what do you want?" I asked him.

"I don't want to scare you but that couple that came to see you a month ago were here tonight. I recognized the old woman's hood and she was with the same old man," Jaxson cried. I could hear my mother laugh, so I knew that she was not far away from me.

"Jaxson, please don't tell my mother or anyone. My mother would freak out," I begged.

"Oh, I won't, Abby. I promise you I won't tell anyone. I know that sometimes I ain't always nice, but I really like you."

"Jaxson, first thing is I like you, too. Second thing, is there ain't no such word as ain't." He and I both laughed. Jaxson wasn't so bad after all.

Chapter 16-"Guess Who's Coming to Dinner?"

It was a few days before Thanksgiving and after school, Katy and I had to come home and get ready for dad's new boss and his wife to come to dinner.

Mom had some fancy smancy Chinese restaurant cater in food. It smelled wonderful. I had to nibble on some Chinese noodles before Mr. and Mrs. St. Claire were to arrive. Mom fixed my hair in a high ponytail with a matching large clip since I obviously hadn't done it to meet her or my dad's standards for Mr. and Mrs. Moneybags. I was expecting to make polite conversation, eat, and then politely excuse myself so that I could put Neils and Andrea on three-way call from my brand new red cell phone.

I was not ready for the big bombshell that was about to go off.

The first little bombshell was Brewer showing up at our house uninvited. He knocked on the door and begged my dad to let him see Katy. Katy screamed that she didn't want to see him anymore. Brewer than began to cry at the door.

"Oh, for goodness sakes," my dad moaned. "Brewer, will you please come back tomorrow and I promise I will personally make Katy sit down and discuss this matter with you, but not tonight. I am having a very important dinner tonight. Do you understand me? Now please come back tomorrow."

Brewer stated that he understood and that he would be back tomorrow.

"What was that all about?" my mother wanted to know. She must have looked incredible because my dad said something mushy to her and how incredibly beautiful she was. And then the doorbell rang.

"I'll get it," said Katy. "It's the St. Claires."

I wasn't sure what happened next. I just know that when Mr. and Mrs. St. Claire walked into the living room my mother screamed.

Chapter 17- "The Big Chill"

My knees almost buckled underneath me when I heard my mother scream. What was it that she screamed? The word mother?

I heard a familiar sound of a cane on our new hardwood floor, so I was really confused. I stood still and motionless.

"Caroline, I have missed you so much. Please don't be angry with me. I want to be a part of your family. You were right. Jacob is a good, no I mean a great man who is incredibly talented and smart. Yes, my husband, Mr. St. Claire is Jacob's boss but Jacob got this job on his own merit. Harry only agreed to meet with him and nothing else. After he met Jacob he was so impressed with him and could not wait to hire him. Please forgive me for all that I said and have done that might have hurt you."

My mother said nothing for what seemed like an eternity and then she burst into tears and ran out of the room. To break the silence I said all I could think to say, "Are you blind, too?" I asked.

"Yes, Abby. I am blind. You and I have the same eye disease. It is an inherited eye disease and I was so sad when you were born that you inherited this condition from me. Your mother and I said some harsh things to each other. Things that I know we both regret. I want to get to know you and be with you and your family. It is my family, too. My name is Grandmother Elizabeth."

"Are you the one who left us the notes in Braille? I questioned.

"Yes, it was me who was following you. Harry tried to help me see you at school one day when that crazy little boy ran after us."

"That's my friend, Jaxson. He's okay once you get to know him." Just then my mother came out of her bedroom. I could tell that she had been crying because of the way her voice and her nose sounded.

"Mother, you had no right to leave those

scary notes to my child. She was scared to death. Are you trying to come back and make everything okay again after all you said?" There was another long painful silence when all of a sudden I heard loud crying again but this time it was coming from the outside. It was Mr. Brains yelling through the door again for Katy to forgive him.

This was one crazy and chilly night.

Chapter 18- "To Forgive is Divine"

My mother immediately ran over to her mother and threw her arms around her. They both started crying and hugging each other.

"Abby looks just like you and she acts just like you, too." Then Brewer let himself in and started crying and begging Katy to forgive him. Katy hugged Brewer and they both started crying.

Dad, Harry St. Claire and I all just stood and waited for the sobbing to stop. We all sat down and ate Chinese food that night. I love the sweet and sour chicken with egg rolls. I asked Grandmother Elizabeth why they didn't make fortune cookies in Braille.

"Hmm," she thought. "Maybe we could start a new trend," she laughed.

Mom and Grandmother Elizabeth talked all night and until early the next morning. I fell asleep in the chair and Dad carried me up to bed. I don't know what all was said between Katy and Einstein but I guess they made up too.

I woke up the next morning with a new grandparent, well, actually two new grandparents. We all really like Harry a lot. He fits in our family well unlike Mr. Rocket Scientist.

Chapter 19- "Thanksgiving Day"

Our whole family was coming over for our Thanksgiving feast: Harry, Grandmother Elizabeth, Grand Pop, Nan, Katy, Mom, Dad, Aunt Blake and me.

I talked to Andrea and Neils on my cell phone while I was still cuddled up in my new bed that surrounded me with soft large pillows.

"It was the craziest night ever," I replied.

"I thought my family was nuts," is how funny Neils responded.

"If you see Jaxson, tell him not to whack my grandparents with Old Man Massey's broom," I laughed.

I got off of the phone and put on my new soft blue velvet jeans and a new blue jean jacket. I brushed my hair and pulled it back into a long ponytail and went quickly downstairs.

Grandmother Elizabeth has a folding cane and the neatest guide dog named Dolly. Dolly is a black Labrador retriever and she is so sweet. My grandmother took off Dolly's harness which lets Dolly know that she's off of work and can play. I cannot wait until I can have my own guide dog. Grandmother Elizabeth and Ms. Harriet said that I have to first be very good with my orientation and mobility skills and graduate from high school. I will then go off and be trained with a puppy at a training school just like my grandmother. She went to New Jersey when she first got Dolly. I played with Dolly all day after we ate our, let's see if I can phrase it like the cafeteria menu, oh, yes, creamy whipped potatoes, with roasted turkey and hot buttered rolls.

We all sat around and watched the Dallas Cowboys beat the Washington Redskins. Harry and Dad were hooting and hollering and giving each other high-fives all during the game while Mom, Grandmother Elizabeth and Nan were all planning a big after Thanksgiving shopping spree. Katy was outside talking to one of our new neighbors. It just happens to be a boy her age, cute and seems like he actually might have a brain.

Eighteen Months Later
Chapter 20- "The Diamond Duo"

It had been over a year since our family had reunited with my grandparents. I love Harry and feel that he is my grandpa, too. Grandmother Elizabeth is incredible. She and I do things together all of the time. Even though her last name is not Diamond we call each other The Diamond Duo because we both have eyes that look like diamonds.

My grandmother helps Madison and me when we are working on a voice output system. Grandmother Elizabeth and I also take monthly trips using a transit system. We also like for funny Aunt Blake to come along with us. My grandmother sometimes makes me call people who drive people who have a visual impairment travel to their jobs and to events. She said that she now has Harry to help out but she wants to be as independent as possible for as long as she can. I love her so much and want to be just like her. I now know how to handle myself even better when family members and friends are not with me because of her.

I could not believe it but it was time for Katy's graduation. Katy is going to some big university in Texas next fall. She took my fingers and showed me how to hook my horns or something like that like the college kids at the University of Texas. She was so excited and kept talking about meeting all kinds of new boys.

After her graduation, we had a big swimming party in our backyard. Mom let me invite Neils, Andrea and Madison to the party.

Chapter 21 - "Graduation Day"

It was graduation day and all chaos was break out. Katy was yelling about her hair, mom was complaining that her dress looked too tight and dad was complaining that we were all going to be late. My mom and dad said that Katy looked so beautiful. Grandmother Elizabeth and I laughed and said that we would just have to take everyone's word for it. Mom said that Katy's long black hair was curled and that she was wearing a beautiful sky blue dress that matched her blue eyes.

When Katy put on her dark blue and white cap and gown, Mom started crying. I heard her say,

"I am so proud of you and sad that you will be going off in the fall to such a big university."

"Mom, don't cry. I'm not going to the grave, I am going to college."

Dad mumbled that we all needed to get into the car before we were late, so we all crammed into the SUV and drove to the graduation.

It was the most boring time that I think that I had ever had. I wished that I had brought something to read, but when the principal of the school called out, "Katherine Elizabeth Diamond" my family went crazy. Grand Pop even brought a cowbell and began ringing it like crazy.

The party afterwards was a blast, and was everything that Katy had hoped it would be and more. We had loud music, great Tex-Mex food from our favorite restaurant, Gonzalez and a huge chocolate butter cream cake.

Dad and mom asked Katy to come out to the front of the house about an hour after the party started. We all walked out with her. I couldn't see what was happening but then I heard a loud honking sound. My parents were giving Katy a brand new car. It was a beautiful black SUV. Katy started screaming and jumping up and down. There was a big red bow tied on top of the car. I was excited for Katy and so proud of her. Afterwards,

Madison, Neils , Andrea and I stayed up late and swam outside in our pool. Later on we were all downstairs watching television, and we heard a noise.

"What's that?" asked Madison.

"Oh, my gosh!" screamed Andrea. "The door knob is turning. Someone is trying to get in."

After a few minutes, which seemed like a lifetime, Neils, being the adventurous and totally insane one in the group, walked outside and found another note.

"I know it's not Grandmother Elizabeth," I firmly stated. "She and Harry left to go on a cruise."

"But, Abby, the note is written in Braille," Andrea told me.

"Let Madison read what it says. I am too nervous." Madison took the note and slid her fingers across the lines of Braille.

"Well, whoever brailled this is not very good at it. It says, 'I liki yuu a lot. Will yuu be ny girlfd." I was so confused and wondered who would leave another Braille note. I could hear everyone talking but Neils.

"Neils, where are you?" I screamed. "Everyone, I can't find Neils. We have to go and look for her."

Just then the door opened and in came Neils dragging someone with her.

"Look who I found outside with the tape he used to tape the note on the door," Neils shook her head.

"Who is it?" I asked.

"Hi Abby. It's me, Jaxson. I ain't never been so embarrassed in my life." We were all so quiet for a moment and then burst out into laughter. Even Jaxson started laughing.

"Well, Jaxson, I don't want a boyfriend now, but I could use another friend. Come on and let's eat some cake before you go home. And Jaxson, there ain't no such word as ain't."

Abby Diamond in...
"Alison- The Fourth Musketeer"

"A lie keeps growing and growing
until it's as plain as the nose on your face"- Pinocchio

"Chapter 1"

Since school started, we were all settling into hanging out with a really cool group of kids. However, as cool as the kids were, no one could get into our closely -knit group, The Three Musketeers, until an unusual girl walked into the classroom.

I'll never forget this particular day when Ms. Ashley and I were finished with our Braille lesson.

I went back into the classroom when I heard Ms. Adams introduce a new girl to the class. Her name was Alison Cash.

I was hanging my cane back on the hook when Alison began spinning a wild tale that was so wild that even I had a hard time believing. This new girl was telling the class that she had previously lived in a mansion and that both of her parents were famous movie stars. She told us that they were in movies all of the time and that they had each won an Academy Award. I heard Jaxson whisper to Neils,

"Then why is she wearing those old dirty rags?"

"Shhh," Neils whispered to him. "Maybe she's lying so that people will like her." After Alison finished embarrassing herself, she sat down and I heard Jaxson call her a liar. She must have ducked her head down to cry because I heard Andrea tell Jaxson to shut his mouth. When Ms. Adams asked Alison to take her seat in front of me, I tapped her on the shoulder and said,

"Hi. My name is Abby. It is nice to meet you."

"Hi," she returned and then added, "Are you blind?"

"Yes," I said. "I have been blind since birth and so has my Grandmother Elizabeth."

"Can you see anything?" she asked.

"No, not much. Just shapes and shadows."

"You are so beautiful," she told me.

"Thank you," I said. "I bet you are, too."

The bell rang and we had to line up to go

to the dreaded lunchroom at our school. The food was hideous; the lunchroom ladies were grouches and yelled at us daily. One time one old grouch with bad breath took me by the hand, made me sit down at the table by myself and served me a plate of ..... I better not finish that sentence. I told Ms. Ashley and boy was she mad. She and I went back into the cafeteria. Ms. Ashley told all of the crows that I was to walk through the line, carry my own tray and make food choices like everyone else does daily.

"But she can't see!" chirped one old lady.

"What was your first clue, Ms. Brains?"

"Abby, you be quiet," scolded Ms. Ashley. Geez I thought that we could gang up on the bullies together.

The next day during lunch, the goofy lunchroom workers allowed me to do what Ms. Ashley had requested but they were not any nicer about it.

"We are serving salad, pizza and peaches," one of the old ladies barked.

"Great, I feel like I am at the Ritz Hotel."

"That blind one has a smart mouth," I overhead one of them say. Unfortunately for her, Andrea and Neils heard it, too. They left the lunch line and went straight to our principal, Mrs. Cummings. Mrs. Cummings is a great principal but she doesn't take anything off of anyone. So, as we were walking with our new buddy, Pinocchio, I mean Alison, we warned her about the lunchroom and its occupants. Even though Alison lies really bad, she was gradually becoming the Fourth Musketeers.

After lunch one day, Andrea, Neil, Alison and I were standing around on the playground waiting on the bell to ring so that we could go back to class for more free education. We were talking about a favorite movie when Alison began talking, I mean lying, nonstop.

"My parents are in that movie," Alison lied. "They are in California this week filming." Andrea, Neils and I became silent and allowed her nose to grow more. I felt like I was listening to a train wreck.

"Yes," Pinocchio continued, "I can't wait for them to come back and get me. They are going to buy me a large house, a big diamond and a swimming pool."

Neils tried to derail the train wreck by saying, "Alison, why don't you come over Friday night and spend the night with us?"

"Sure," she muttered. "I'll have to let my

father know, but I'm sure that it will be okay."

Alison continued more tales of her times in Hollywood with her mother and dad. She told us that her mother had been in over twenty movies and was only twenty-eight years old. After Alison walked off, I said to Neils and Andrea,

"Why is she lying so bad? I wish that she would stop it and let us know the truth about her home."

"Something's up," Andrea replied. "There's no way that she has any money. Her clothes don't fit and are dirty. Why does she think that being rich will make us like her better? I really like her," Andrea went on, "until she starts all of her bogus lying." Bogus, I thought. I like that new word and will try to use it the next chance I get.

"Fun Friday"

FRIDAY- I love it when you are sitting in class on a Friday afternoon waiting on the freedom bell to ring. Tonight was our slumber party at Neil's house. I love to go to Neil's house because Mr. and Mrs. Roberts are great cooks and according to what I feel when I hug them, they enjoy everything that they cook.

The Roberts are truly two of the nicest people that I have ever met.

I was in the middle of my daydream about the Roberts' homemade pizza when I heard Liar, Liar, Pants on Fire, firing off her lies again during our geography lesson.

"My parents and I rode on a camel once. Then the three of us went on a safari," Alison lied.

"That's nice, Alison," Ms. Adams said.

"But I do need to get back to my lesson."

When the bell finally rang, Alison chirped,

"See you girls tonight."

"I like Alison," Neils said. "But I am sick of listening to all of her lies. We need to be frank with her and ask for the truth. We will reassure her that we really like her for who she is and not for her so-called famous parents."

That night we were all at Neil's house munching on cheese dip, chips and eating homemade pizza with the Roberts when the doorbell rang.

"Maybe that is Alison," said Neils. To our dismay, it was the boy next door waiting to be invited to eat pizza with Neil's three brothers. Neils is the only girl in her family, but she knows how to handle herself. Her three brothers tease her a lot but I can also tell how protective they are of her. I can't blame the intruder for busting in on our party because I always love to listen to Mrs. Roberts' big booming laugh, visit with this fun-loving family and eat big greasy meals.

"How is Katy?" Mrs. Roberts wanted to know.

"Great. She has a new boyfriend that actually has a brain." Everyone laughed hysterically because they knew Old Dumb-dumb (Brewer) from the neighborhood.

Later that night, we spread out our sleeping bags and began talking about Alison.

"Something is up with her and her family situation," Andrea said. "I wonder if she lives alone or has really bad parents."

"She obviously needs help, attention or something like that," I added.

Neils responded, "Let's follow her home one day without her knowing."

"Not a bad idea, and then we can see the best way to help her out," Andrea replied.

We stayed up late playing cards. Yes, a blind kid gets to join in. They always let me bring my Braille playing cards, so I can join in on the fun, too, on any card game. The next morning, Mrs. Roberts made us homemade biscuits with hot butter and honey.

I had so much fun that I wasn't ready to leave around 10:00 that morning when my mom came to pick me up. I was telling my mom about our concerns for Alison when Mom told me to keep her updated on any new information. She had seen Alison in the hallway and had noticed how unkempt she looked.

"Abby, find out what you can about Alison, so I can follow up. I may need to talk to our school counselor about her." I promised that I would and then we both drove home silently while deep in thought.

"Texas School for the Blind"

Every year at least twice during the school year, my parents take Madison and me to the School for the Blind for a week of learning technology skills, recreation and leisure and other skills that help us so that we are more successful in life. I love my time spent down in Austin. When Madison and I attend the camp, we always get to bunk together in our own dorm room. I always feel like I am in college like Katy.

We have dorm parents who are there with us, too. They help us to do our homework and any other needs that we might have. I love my school and of course my best buddies from school, but there is still nothing like attending this camp with others who have a visual impairment.

We sit around with the teachers, who like Ms. Ashley are awesome. After we learn our skills, we go swimming, shopping and many other great activities. On Friday before we leave to go back to our regular schools, we have a big pizza party.

I especially enjoy the socialization time because I have a crush on a boy that is older than I am named Brock. Brock lost his vision when he was a baby from an infection or something like that. He is really cool. He competes in our Sports Extravaganza and wins all of the trophies and medals. I heard my sister, Katy once comment that she wished that he was older because he was gorgeous; I really like his personality. I mean, it doesn't feel sorry for himself or anything like that. He just wins awards and is a straight 'A' student. One time Brock told me that he was going to be a research doctor and cure cancer one day.

My heart was beating so fast.... I hoped no one could notice my face blush. However, I must not have been doing too good of a job hiding my feelings because one day Madison started teasing me.

"You love Brock. Brock and Abby sitting in a tree k-i-s-s-i-n-g first comes love then comes marriage then comes Abby with a baby carriage." We laughed so hard. I grabbed her and started playfully tackling her. Our dorm mother, who is a college girl named Kandi, was cracking up, too.

"OOOh, Abby loves Brock," Kandi continued.

"You girls better to get to Mrs. Smith's class or you'll get me in trouble. Now scoot." We both took off running to class and laughing hysterically. The funny thing about her last sentence is that Mrs. Jamie Smith is the sweetest vision teacher at the school. Madison and I just love her. She makes us work hard on our reading and writing skills, but she is really cool.

Mrs. Smith asked us to write about someone that we admire or really like. Keep it in our note taker, do spell check and then print it out. I already had my prompt in mind. I was going to write about Brock and how much I admired his ambition to become a doctor and how he doesn't let any obstacle get in the way of what he truly wants. I wanted to add, 'I wish that he wanted me,' but of course I didn't do that. Madison and I were sitting and typing when I heard the worst news ever, Brock had a girlfriend who was driving and going to pick him Friday. The old man-stealer was going to eat pizza with us according to Erin, a friend of mine who also attended the school with us.

"No," I whispered quietly to Madison when she and I both overhead Erin talking to Ms. Smith.

"Abby, I don't know what you look like, but I have heard that you are very pretty. I bet that she isn't as pretty as you are," Madison said quietly.

"Thanks, Madison, but I think that you think that because we are friends." Even though I got the bad news about the boyfriend stealer coming down to see Brock, we continued to have the best time.

We went swimming one day, and Brock began throwing Madison and me around while we laughed hysterically. He was so great and so funny, but there was only one little obstacle that I had to take care of I thought. Abby Diamond is typically a good girl, doesn't make waves and tries to make peace but this was war. Rarely did I like confrontation but I can take care of myself and my future husband. I mean, he and I are the perfect couple. I mean we have so much in common and could be Mr. and Mrs. Brock...? I need to find out his last name before I finish that sentence.

It was finally Friday and I had my plan ready for the intruder who was in the way of my future dreams and children.

Mrs. Smith and Mrs. Armand gathered us all together in the lunchroom for our party.

I was listening and waiting for the intruder to come prancing in, listen to her squawking laughter and then I was going to make my bad girl moves. I mean, I had to get back my boyfriend. Okay, he isn't exactly my boyfriend. We all gathered around the tables while many people coming into the room. My parents were actually going to arrive towards the end of our party because of my dad's job, so I didn't have a clue who was coming into the room.

I was struggling to figure out which pizza I wanted when one of the nicest people that I have ever met began helping me. I mean, she was so cool. We started laughing and talking about our schools. She said that she went to a high school not too far from this campus. She also told me that she was going to attend The University of Texas during the fall semester. I squealed and told her that my sister Katy was there.

My new friend and I sat down together and ate pizza. Everyone was talking and laughing and then it was time to go. I heard my mom from across the room. She really misses me when I am gone.

"Abby, I'm over here," she yelled. She ran and threw her arms around me and then I could smell my dad's cologne. I felt his large hairy arms reach around and grab me. I felt so much love and had missed them so much. Mom, Dad and I were walking back to the dorm when my new friend walked up to me.

"Abby, it was great to meet you. I promise you that I will look up Katy next year."

"Nice to meet you, too," I said. "I hope to see you again sometime."

"You bet," she said. And then I heard words that broke my heart.

"Come on Brock, let's get started, we got a party to go to tonight."

"FOOD FIGHT!"

The next Monday morning after my week at camp, Ms. Ashley was helping me access the Internet through a voice output system. I give the keyboard commands and the man's robotic voice begins to speak whatever a sighted person sees. My Grandmother Elizabeth and I work together on the Internet, too, so I am getting really good at it.

"Great work, Abby," Ms. Ashley beamed. "You are going to take all of the awards away from the other children at Technology Camp." She and I both laughed because as skilled as I am getting on technology there are many of the other kids who are as good if not better than I am in technology skills.

Ms. Ashley sent me back to class and it was time for lunch. Usually this is a kid's favorite time of a school day unless you happen to be in our cafeteria. Even my mom said one time that Mrs. Cummings is not happy with the way the ladies treat us sweet and innocent children.

"Don't hold up the line," one of the lunchroom ladies hollered at me.

"Sorry, I accidentally left my eye sight at home," I retorted. Neils, Andrea and Jaxson burst out laughing, clapping, hooting and hollering. Next thing I knew the four of us were being escorted to the discipline table. To add insult to injury, the winch told my mother on me.

My mother politely told the lunchroom meanie that while she didn't approve of my rudeness, she would still appreciate more patience with me traveling through the line because of my disability. For retaliation, because the old grouches were mean to the blind kid, Moi, several of the sixth grade boys began throwing food at the old bats. Mrs. Cummings and Coach Johnson came running into the lunchroom and hauled them off to the office.

Andrea and Neils were laughing so hard because, according to them, the old cronies had luscious whipped potatoes and ripened peaches dripping from their hairnets.

"Mystery Man"

The next day I was sitting in the classroom alone while waiting on my class to return from music when I heard footsteps entering the room.

"Who's there?" I said, but nobody answered me. The footsteps quickly left the classroom, but not before I heard glass or something being placed on a table. Shortly after that, our class came back inside the room. Everyone began "ooing and aahing".

"Abby, do you know who left these here?" Ms. Adams asked.

"Left what?" I asked.

"This beautiful vase filled with red roses."

"I heard someone come in but they didn't answer me when I asked who it was. "Hmmm,"

Ms. Adams said, " the note says: 'Have a wonderful day. The roses do not compare to your beauty.'

"Wow!" our class said.

"Sorry, Ms. Adams. I wish that I could give you more information. I heard loud footsteps and smelt a man's really strong cologne."

"Poor Little Rich Girl"

One day after school was out for the weekend, Mom told me that Katy was home for the next few days. I don't admit this to many people, but I had missed Katy so much since she had been away at college. When Mom and I drove up in the driveway, I could hear Katy yell my name.

"Abby, I have missed you so much!" She hugged me so tight that I could barely breathe.

"Me, too," I choked.

That night Dad, Mom, Nan, Pop, Harry and Grandmother Elizabeth and I were eating ribs that Dad had cooked out on the grill. Mom and I began talking about the new girl, Alison.

"I hope that she isn't being abused," Nan said with concern in her voice."

"Abby, I'm going to be home through next Tuesday so why don't you, Neil, Andrea and I follow Alison home without her knowing it. We'll see where she lives and who lives with her," Katy said.

"Great idea, Katy. I am so worried about Alison and really want to be friends with her, but I can't be friends with her but I can't stand listening to all of her bogus lies all of the time." The rest of the weekend was really fun. All of the girls went shopping for clothes. Since we didn't have to watch every red cent, I really got into shopping just like Nan. I couldn't wait to wear my new dark jeans that had tactual designs on the back. After we left, the mall my Mom said, "Abby, why don't you see if Alison would like some of the clothes that you no longer wear? She's really small for her age."

"Sure, Mom, but I have to be careful that she doesn't feel like a charity case." We pulled over and went to a favorite fast food joint. I always get the vanilla ice cream cone regardless of the Flavor of the Day.

The following Monday after school, Neils,

Andrea, Katy and I all piled into Katy's SUV and followed the school bus.

"Everyone describe to me what you're seeing," I begged.

"Abby, we haven't seen anything yet but streets and cars," Katy said. Just then the bus took a sharp left and then an immediate right.

"Oh, no," Andrea said. "It's worse than I thought. Abby, we are looking at an old boarded-up shack. I see Alison using her key to go inside of one of the worst looking houses that I had ever seen."

Andrea began explaining more to me, "The paint is all peeling off, there's an old bicycle with rust all over it and porch looks like it's going to cave in."

I couldn't help it. I began to cry. Just like that. I started crying. I wanted to run inside of the old shack and rescue Alison.

"Abby, don't cry," said Neils. "We will get her help. We just have to see what is going on inside of this old house."

Tuesday morning I heard Alison come into the room.

"Hey Alison. I have several clothes that no longer fit would you like them?"

"Oh, thanks, but I don't know where I could

put them. I have so many expensive clothes that I'm not allowed to wear to school." Oh, brother. Pinocchio was at it again.

"But, I may know of someone poor who could use them."

"Alison that would be great. You would really be helping me out. Why don't you call your parents, and see if you can come over after school. My mom can take you home afterwards."

"Well, could you bring them in a bag to school tomorrow? I have ballet lessons tonight."

I began, "Sure that would be great. And Alison, I am really that we are friends even if you didn't have movie star parents."

"My Brother's Keeper"

I brought Alison the clothes the following day. I could tell that she was happy by the excitement in her voice. But, of course, she had to save face by adding,

"I know of a poor little girl who could wear these."

I guess Alison felt saying all of this to me because she knew that I couldn't see. To be truthful, since my dad was making the big bucks, I had so many clothes that no one would probably notice that the new clothes that she was wearing were actually mine.

When the bell rang to begin school the next morning, I heard Jaxson whisper, "Alison must have burned her old rags because she's wearing new jeans and a white sweater with white fur." I smiled to myself. I loved that sweater and I hoped that Alison would like it, too.

That night Andrea and her mother were coming home from church when Andrea asked her mother to take a detour and go by Alison's house to check on her. Mrs. Williams and Andrea drove by the decrepit old shack and could see Alison still wearing her white sweater with the fur pouring a bowl of cereal. Andrea recognized the sweater earlier in the day that Alison was wearing. Abby is such a sweet and caring person, Andrea thought. When the Williams' drove back by the shack, Andrea saw Alison spill the milk on her sweater. She quickly ran to the sink and began frantically scrubbing the milk off of her sweater.

"Where are her parents?" Ms. Williams wanted to know.

"In Hollywood," chirped Andrea.

"What?" Mrs. Williams asked.

"Never mind, Mom, it's a long story." Mrs. Williams continued, "I'm calling Abby's mom tomorrow and ask her to talk to the school counselor and principal to see what's going on with this child."

Alison was alone and she was miserable. I miss my dad so much at night she was thought.

I wish that he wasn't so tired when he came walking in around midnight every night, but of course he had to help clean up before the next day. Alison turned on the television and tried to watch some dumb new reality show but it was just silly. She had already done her homework and was sitting and staring at the wall alone again. I love my new friends, she thought. I just wish that I lived with one of them and then I wouldn't be here alone all of the time with all of my sad thoughts.

I miss my mother, so when my dad is gone to the diner, I sit and cry and stare at her picture. She and I really resemble, and people think that I sing just like she does. I can't show Audie, my dad, how much I miss her because he always feels so sorry for me. I feel sorry for me too, tonight.

"More Flowers"

Wednesday morning when I walked into my classroom, I was knocked out by the smell of more flowers that had been placed all over our classroom by Ms. Adams's secret admirer.

I was teasing Andrea and told her that I thought Ms. Adams's secret admirer was Mr. Massey, our custodian. Andrea guessed Mr. Bishop the man who delivers our milk to the school. His wife's name is Beth. They live down the street from us and are really great people.

"Andrea, Mr. Bishop is already married to Beth. Besides that fact, his wife his beautiful with her short stylish haircut and great big beautiful green eyes," Neils replied.

She guessed the crossing guard, Old Man Bernie.

"Great guess," retorted Jaxson. Bernie is one hundred years old and Ms. Adams is twenty. Great match."

"Shut up, Jaxon," yelled Neils.

Neils described a purple and red bouquet of flowers and several mixes of daisies and other beautiful flowers.

"Everyone settle down," Ms. Adams said. "It's time for writing."

I loved to write so this was my favorite time of the day. I liked how Ms. Adams gave us story starters and let us create. She was also great to not make us feel like losers even when some of the kids who must be completely nuts to write some of the dumb stuff that they wrote. Sometimes what the kids wrote and read aloud was hysterical to me, but I enjoy being friends with everyone, so I keep my trap shut.

Ms. Adams, like my Aunt Blake, says that I have a true gift for writing. They both keep talking to me about having my writings published one day. They think that one day I could become a published author.

Thursday afternoon Ms. Adams was called to the office while I was gathering my materials. I smelled the familiar cologne and heard the footsteps entering the classroom.

"Who's there?" I asked. No one answered. I spoke louder this time, "Stop scaring my teacher, you psycho." I heard a man chuckle and then leave the room and then five minutes later, Ms. Adams came back into the room.

"More flowers?" she questioned.

"Ms. Adams, it's the same cologne and big feet that came in again today. And," I continued, "He wears too much cologne."

Ms. Adams laughed and said, "Well, that leaves out Mr. Massey." We both laughed and walked out of the classroom together arm-in arm.

"Guess Who?"

The mysterious flowers continued and no one had any idea who was behind the mystery until gym class one morning. Neils took me to Coach Johnson's office to ask him for a beep ball. A beep ball is a ball for the blind that beeps when you turn it on. My sighted friends love to play with it too during our free time in the gym. Neils and I walked into Coach Johnson's office and then it hit me!

Friday afternoon when my class was in art class, Ms. Ashley took me back to my class early so that she could talk to Ms. Adams about something. She told me to work on spell check on my note taker. After Ms. Ashley left the room, I heard the footsteps and smelt the strong cologne.

"Hi Coach Johnson," I smiled.

"Abby. How did you know it was me?" he chuckled. "Strong cologne, Coach," I laughed. "But don't worry Coach, your secret is safe with me."

"Well," Coach Johnson continued, "Since I've been caught, it may be time for me to tell Cathy, I mean Ms. Adams." I hate mushy stuff, so when Cathy, I mean Ms. Adams walked into the room I asked to go to the bathroom. It must have worked out great because three months later, we were all invited to Ms. Adams and Coach Johnson's wedding.

Another confrontation was about to take place between Alison and The Three Musketeers.

"Alison, my mom and I saw you alone the other night. We know where you live and we want to continue to be friends with you, but we will not tolerate any more lies," Andrea said sternly. Alison stood their motionless and then what seemed an eternity, she finally spoke.

"I live alone with my dad. His name is Audie Cash and he's a cook at the local diner. My mother passed away three years ago of a horrible disease. I love to talk about my famous movie star parents because it helps me to not feel so lonely." It was our turn to stand motionless.

"Alison, we're here for you," I said. "Why don't you come home with me, spend the night and then go to school tomorrow with my mother and me. My mom will call and ask your dad for you." Alison agreed and called Audie immediately, and he seemed thrilled that Alison was not going to be alone another night while he worked at the diner.

That afternoon Mom took Alison and me shopping. She bought Alison a flat iron for her long brown hair, two pair of jeans, four really cool shirts, a pair of tennis shoes, a pair of black boots and another great pair of brown ones. I could hear how excited Alison was. When she thanked my mom, I could hear my mom's voice quiver.

"Alison, why don't you stay with us during the week at night? You can ride to school with Abby and me every morning." Alison squealed with cheers and so did I.

"Oh, boy. I've missed my sister so much and now I'm getting another one," I beamed.

"Audie"

The lunchroom was getting worse. Mrs. Cummings was getting ready to fire them, according to my mother. The ladies, if I have to call them that, were meaner by the day and the food tasted like old dog food. Mom called Audie one day and they talked for hours.

She found out that Audie was a great cook and that he and Alison had gone through some really bad times financially the past few years. The only job that he could get in a smaller town was one at the diner cooking and working the night shift. He was waiting on a day-shift job to open up for him and Alison, so that he could be with her at night.

I was shocked to hear what they talked about next. Mom talked to Mrs. Cummings about hiring Audie to be our cook and to help and manage our disastrous lunchroom. Come to find out, Audie and Mrs. Cummings hit it off instantly, and the next thing I knew, Audie was wearing a hairnet and managing the lunchroom.

The mood in the cafeteria had already begun to change. What a difference one person can make. Audie was smiling and talking to the kids and was very patient with the blind kid, Yours Truly. I heard him politely correct the cranky women when they were prone to rudeness, but he always did it with kindness and respect.

Another day he said, "Now Agnes, the kid is only five-years-old. Let's give him a break." Even the cafeteria meanies were responding to him. He joked with them and had them eating out of his hands within a matter of days. Audie began changing the menu and when it read ripened peaches and creamy whipped potatoes it was no longer a piece of fiction.

Alison stopped spending the weekday nights with me because Audie was able to be at home with her. They even moved to a better place down the street from where we used to live.

"I feel like I live at the Taj Mahal," Alison beamed to me one day. Awesome Audie was really getting into his new job and brilliant at it. He redecorated the cafeteria, had contest among the classes and began cooking more delicious and healthy meals. The superintendent of our schools made a special visit to see "Awesome Audie's Cafeteria".

Alison's lies suddenly stopped and she was suddenly becoming the fourth musketeer. I could hear happiness in her voice that I had never heard before. She also has a terrific laugh, and I bet that she can sing great when she wants.

"Spring Break"

It was time for our spring break and I was getting so excited because my family was going to Sea World in San Antonio, Texas. I was even more excited because Katy was going, too. For the first time in a long time, The Fab Four was going to be together for a few days of fun.

My dad always yells for everyone to go to the bathroom before we pull out in our SUV with all of our luggage and ice chests full of sodas and food. Dad loves for everyone to eat and have a great time. We were finally ready to go. As much as we couldn't wait to be together, we hadn't been in the car any longer than forty-five minutes when Katy had to go to the bathroom, and we were already on each other's nerves. Dad popped off and asked Katy why she hadn't gone earlier. We finally arrived to our hotel. I guess you could say that it was a fancy smancy hotel. They even left us chocolate mints on our pillow. I ate Katy's and my yummy chocolate.

The next morning we put on our shorts because it is really warm in San Antonio and drove to Sea World. It was a blast. Even though I couldn't see what was going on, my dad made sure that I didn't miss what was going on during the shows. We rode a roller coaster ride that Mom said was in the shape of Shamu, the killer whale. I don't know what Shamu looks like, but I know that he must really be big because I could hear a huge splash every time he landed in the water.

Katy took me down to the splash zone where we were drenched. Shamu splashed us really hard several times. I could hear the crowd scream and clap when we were splashed over and over again. Katy and I laughed so hard and so did Mom and Dad.

We went and ate at the restaurant there and ate hot dogs, fries and I got a huge soda that was in a container shaped like a killer whale. We saw the dolphins, too. Yes, I can see, but I "see" with my hands. The dolphins would swim up to me and I could feel their slick cold skin. Even though it was warm, it was still a little chilly for us to go to the water park, but Mom promised us that we could go next time. We closed down the park and were all so tired when we got back to the hotel that we all feel immediately asleep.

The next day was a blast, too, sort of. We went to the Mexican Market place where I bought a smooth Mexican doll that I named Maria, and ate Mexican food at an infamous restaurant named Mi Tiara's. We also walked on the River Walk. The River Walk is known for its beauty. We took a ride on a water boat and rode through the canals. When I was getting off of the boat with help from my dad, I remembered that I had left Maria on the boat.

"Dad, I have to go back for Maria," I screamed. "Who the heck is Maria?" My dad asked.

"My doll," I yelled back.

Then something happened that would be the talk of people who were there for many years to come. The boat had moved slightly away from where I was standing and I fell into the river. Next thing I knew my dad had jumped into the water to save me. People were screaming, "The girl fell into the water!"

The workers helped pull Dad and me out of the murky water.

"Senorita, here is your doll," one nice man said

to me. Everyone felt so sorry for me. They brought me towels, hot tea for Dad and me and asked if we wanted a free ride on the boat. Dad politely declined and we went back to the hotel laughing really loud in our car. I have to say that Maria was worth it. Even though she caused me to fall in the river and she still smells like paint.

"Maria"

We had a really great time in San Antonio during our spring break. Neils told me that she stayed home and slept late every day and Andrea said that she went snow skiiing. Alison was equally content to have stayed home and slept in. Even though we all had such a great time being out of town with our families, The Four Musketeers were happy to be back at school together. I told my friends about me falling into the river and they ripped roar laughing. Neils laughed so hard that she actually started to choke.

"Oh, no, Abby!" "You didn't. Did you?" squealed Andrea.

"Yes, and I did it all for my little doll who still smells like paint." After we talked about our spring break the bell rang and we went back to class. Ms. Adams, the newly engaged Ms. Adams I might add, was really boring us today with her constant talk of prepositional phrases and how they add to our sentences to make them more developed and elaborate.. There's one kid in the class, Glen who really had a hard time with this concept or he just wanted attention. Mrs. Adams went on and on and on and Glen just kept saying, "Huh? I don't get it."

It was later that night and I had fallen fast asleep. After that boring English lesson and the San Antonio trip, I was really tired. All of a sudden, I heard a whisper in my ear.

" A a a a b b b b b b y . AAAAAAABBBBBYYYYYYY. Wake up."

"Who's there?" I called out loudly.

"It's me, Maria." I could smell the fresh paint on Maria's face and could feel her right in my face.

"But, but, you're a doll. You are not real," I muttered.

"Yes, I am. It was funny when you fell into the river. Hahahahahhahahaha," her evil laughter continued.

"No," I screamed. "You are just a doll. You

did not have anything to do with me falling into the river."

"Yes, I did. I only wish that your dad hadn't jumped in to save you," she moaned. I jumped up as quickly as I could and grabbed her around the throat. Then I heard loud laughter. What was going on? The laughter got louder. It was my class. I had fallen asleep again. Ms. Adams was trying not to laugh when she began speaking,

"Abby, I know that you know your prepositions but will you try to stay awake when you're bored? You can really have some nightmares, Girl. By the way, who is Maria," Ms. Adams wanted to know.

That afternoon when I got home from school, I packed Maria into an old shoebox and asked my mom to ship her off to California to my cousin, Brooklyn.

"Here Comes the Bride"

Three months later, I was getting dressed for Ms. Adams and Coach Johnson's wedding. My parents were going to The University of Texas to visit Katy, so I was going to the wedding and spend the weekend with Alison and Audie. My mom fixed my hair in long spiral curls. I had on a short tight black skirt and purple silk shirt with black-heeled sandals. When Audie and Alison saw me, Audie whistled. I cracked up and told him that he was dumb. I asked Audie to tell me what Alison had on.

"Well, she looks just like her mother. She's wearing what I call a baby doll dress. It's light blue and matches her eyes."

"Dad, stop embarrassing me," Alison laughed. "Abby, feel of my new necklace that

Dad bought me. It's baby blue and matches my dress. Feel of my new hoop earrings."

Alison, Audie and I drove to the wedding in Audie's old pick-up truck. We laughed and talked the whole way to the church. The wedding of the year was spectacular. The whole school was practically there. Neils and Andrea told me about the beautiful lavender and cream -colored flowers. Even old Jaxson showed up in a suit.

"Don't nobody say nothing about my suit on Monday," he quipped.

"We won't," Neils chirped. "But, Jaxson, promise us that you will not skip out on English class ever." We all laughed so hard at that one.

The wedding was a blast. Mrs. Cummings pulled up in a charcoal BMWx5. She was dressed to kill dressed in her Chanel beige suit with large buttons that ran down her back. There was dancing, music and a delicious fruit vanilla bride's cake, but my favorite was the creamy chocolate groom's cake. I heard all of the single ladies reaching for the bouquet that the newly Mrs. Johnson was throwing when I heard one bridesmaid cry because she didn't catch the bouquet.

She reminded me of my whiny Aunt Dana. I walked over to Mr. and Mrs. Johnson.

"Tell my about your dress," I squealed.

"It's the color a marshmallow and it doesn't have straps. Feel of my veil, Abby. It is also white. Can you feel of the lace?" I could hear the happiness in her voice.

After the wedding, I spent a fun weekend with Audie and Alison. Audie made us my favorite breakfast, toasted waffles covered with peanut butter and topped with marshmallows.

"The New Boy"

Monday morning we were all sitting in class and chatting about the wedding of the year with our substitute, Mrs. Self. Mrs. Self told us that the happy couple would be in Hawaii for the next week. I left the classroom and went to work with Ms. Ashley. When I came back into the room Mrs. Self was introducing a new boy to the class.

"Class, this is Bryce. Bryce why don't you tell us a little bit about yourself."

"Well," Bryce began, "I might as well be up front about something. My parents are both famous movie stars and have been in several movies."

"OH, NO," the class moaned.

"Not again," I said.

"Really, they are Mr. and Mrs. Oscar

Night," the new kid said. All of a sudden, the classroom door opened and in walked one of the biggest movie stars of our time.

"Son, you forgot your lunch money," Mr. Movie Star said. The girls and Mrs. Self screamed and the boys began high-fiving each other. After the excitement died down, Bryce, the new boy sat down next to Alison.

"Hey, Alison right? Don't I know you from somewhere? Don't our parents run around together?"

My mouth dropped open.

Abby Diamond In... "Double Trouble"

Sometimes the questions are complicated
and the answers are simple-Dr. Seuss

"Welcome Back"

During the last week of school at the end of our fifth grade year, a new boy came to school, Bryce, who is the real son of famous movie stars.

He saw Alison and called her by name. She ducked her head and denied knowing him. He really likes her; I can tell, but the feelings are not mutual. Bryce continued to talk to her that day.

Bryce said, "Alison, your mother's name is Kaitlyn. Don't you remember when our mother's took us to the Bahamas?"

"No," Alison had said abruptly, "You have me mixed up with someone else."

"No, Alison. Remember your mom was hilarious. The island lady let your mom wear her fruit basket on her head? My mom laughed so hard and took pictures of her. I'll bring the pictures if you want."

"Stop saying that my mother is Kaitlyn!" Alison said in a rude tone and stomped out of the room.

It was and is always really hot during the month of August in Texas. Actually, it is down right miserable, but instead of going inside of the building the 'cool' kids were hanging outside. "Let the little ones go inside," Neils barked. Bryce agreed and laughed. Bryce was in our class. He was a great guy, but anytime he tried to speak to Alison, she would walk away.

It was the early fall and this weekend it was time for me to go for one of the fall programs at the Texas School for the Blind. I could not wait to see Madison and of course, Brock. The good news was that he had broken up with his girlfriend. The bad news was that he still thought of me as just a kid. I mean we are only five years apart. When he is ninety, I'll be eighty-five and we can take care of each other in our wheelchairs along with our future children. I have already named our children. I know that I am getting ahead of myself, but I have to plan my life as a future doctor's wife. Our children will be: Carrie, David, Elle and Frederick. That way, we will be A for Abby, B for Brock, C for Caden , D for David, E for Elle, and F for Frederick. I need to rethink Frederick's name because he will be a doctor like his dad.

I was completely going away mentally into my beautiful daydream when I heard Brock say to Madison and me,

"Come on, Kids, let's go swimming." I'll show him who's not a kid one day when I am really not one.

After my week at camp was over, I spent the night with Neils. Mrs. Roberts made us hot cheese dip with sausage and chips, hot gooey cookies, and other great junk to eat. Later on, Neils, her brothers and some of their friends, Andrea, Alison and I played Beep Ball. Everyone has to wear a blindfold so that it keeps the playing field fair for the blind kid, Yours Truly. You divide the teams into two. Equal number of players faces each other yards apart while everyone gets ready to play on their knees. One person rolls the beeping ball really hard while the other team blocks the ball with their body.

The object is to not allow the ball to pass through the line of people. The boys could really roll the ball hard, but they were no match for Neils. Growing up with three brothers has taught her something for sure. It didn't matter when it got really dark because we were playing under blindfold anyway. We had a great time even though we lost.

After a night of beep ball, The Four Musketeers began spreading out the sleeping bags, and we began talking about Bryce. Even though he was the son of famous movie stars, he was the coolest kid and not stuck up at all. I mean, he was really a nice kid, and he was really good-looking. I believe that he had the I- Really- Like- Alison- Blues, but when anyone mentioned his name, she made a grunt sound and according to Andrea she would roll her eyes.

"Don't roll them too hard, Alison they might stick." I said.

Andrea laughed so hard and said,

"Abby, you are a crazy and funny girl." She thinks I'm hilarious even when I am not really that funny. I innocently told Alison that I thought Bryce really liked her and wanted to know why she didn't like him as a friend.

She said simply, "Because he reminds me of the times that I was telling everyone all of the terrible lies. I finally told the truth, everybody believed me and now he starts it all over again."

I quickly changed the subject and began talking about a new place at the mall called "Sydney and Brandt's", S&D for short. They had the best jewelry and I loved their earrings. I also told my friends about my mom's twin sister, Emma and her daughter, Brooklyn.

"Mom and Aunt Emma look exactly and since Brooklyn looks just like her mom, and I look just like my mom, we also look like twins."

"I didn't know that your mom has a twin. That is so cool," Andrea said. "How come she can come here and not be in school if she's our age?" she wanted to know.

"They live in California where there is year-round school, so they will be off for one of their breaks," I told them. "

"Wow, I'm moving to California," Neils laughed.

"The beach is great is Southern California," Alison said.

"How do you know?" asked Neils.

"Oh, Audie and I went one summer and had a great time."

After we stayed up really late laughing and talking, we all fell asleep- Except for Alison and me.

"Brooklyn"

I had not 'seen' my look-a-like cousin, Brooklyn in three years.

My mom, Katy and I flew to California and stayed with Brooklyn, my Aunt Emma, and her little brother Michael Andrew.

We were both nine years old at the time. We had such a great time together. Everyone kept commenting on how much we looked alike as well as how much our mothers resembled, too. We were the four twins. People would stop, stare and point at the four of us because we all looked so much alike. Katy said that she and Michael Andrew stood out because they had almost black hair to our very blonde hair.

I really liked Brooklyn a lot. She took me by

the hand and we swam with our twin mothers closely by in the freezing cold ocean water.

"Here, Abby. Take my hand and we'll jump over the waves together," Brooklyn once said.

We jumped the waves, swam underneath the water with our life vest on and built a sand castle together.

She was my favorite cousin of them all, so when I had that nightmare dream about my Mexican doll, Maria, I wanted Maria to have a good home, but not with me, so I sent her to live with Brooklyn.

I remember that the six of us also went to Universal Studios in Los Angeles. You can go to the studio and see how the movies are made. Brooklyn carefully described everything to me, so that I could enjoy the sounds at the studio. My Aunt Emma bought all of the kids matching shirts from the beach. Brooklyn and I called them our best friend shirts.

I hadn't talked to or seen Brooklyn in a long time, but I overheard my mom telling my dad that my Aunt Emma and her husband Paul were getting a divorce. She said that Paul had left California and moved to the other side of the country wherever that is. I think that Aunt Emma was pretty sad about everything, so she thought that bringing the kids to Texas would be a nice break for them.

"Well, at least Emma doesn't have to worry about money," I heard Mom say to Dad.

"She has always been the bread-winner around the house and makes even more money now than ever."

"Money isn't everything," Dad said and Mom agreed.

"Evil Twin"

At the beginning of the school year, it is really hard to get back into the groove although I feel excitement at the start of a new grade. My new teacher's name is Mrs. Meers. Mrs. Meers is a great teacher, but she works us really hard. Ms. Ashley said that it is because Mrs. Meers is trying to get us ready for middle school. My stomach hurts when I think of middle school, but I have another year before that happens.

Emily, Neils, Alison, Andrea and I were outside during PE in the very very hot Texas sun playing a game of Four Square with my beep ball. Emily began talking about how much she liked Bryce and how nice he was. She said that she and a couple of other kids went to his house over the weekend. Emily also said that he had a really big house with a huge swimming pool and a tennis court. All of the kids stayed at Bryce's and played for hours.

"Everyone will have to come with us the next time that we go to Bryce's house," she said.

"No thanks!" Alison chirped.

"What's wrong with Bryce," Emily wanted to know.

"He keeps thinking that I am someone that he once knew. He won't let it drop and I am sick of it."

"Well, he's nice to me," Emily stated firmly.

Thankfully, I heard the bell ring and walked with Andrea to get my cane.

"Alison acts too weird about Bryce," I said.

"She sure does. I think something's up and we're going to find out what," Andrea said.

That afternoon when I got home from school, I could hear the Bobsy twins, my mom and aunt, talking and laughing when I walked through the door.

"Abby's here," Aunt Emma squealed.

"Hi Aunt Emma. I'm so glad you're here," I screamed. She gave me a big hug and a huge wet kiss. I really love my mother's sisters so much. Aunt Blake and Aunt Emma are the best.

"Where's Brooklyn?" I wanted to know.

"She's upstairs looking around your room. And Abby. I am so glad that you are living in Mom's house."

"Thanks Aunt Emma. I do, too."

I walked up the stairs to my room, went in and heard Brooklyn playing music on my new iPod.

"Hey, Brooklyn. I'm so glad to see you."

"Likewise," is all Brooklyn said.

Her voice really sounded different from when we were nine years old. She sounded like she had an attitude working.

"So how is school?" I asked.

"Nunya," she said.

"Huh? Nunya?" I questioned.

"Yeah, nunya business."

I felt my face grow red and angry. What an attitude I thought. I didn't know what to say next. I just sat there stunned and felt as though I had been slapped in the face hard.

I mean, I had loved her so much the last time that I had seen her and now she was acting like someone else. Someone mean.

"Well, I'll be downstairs if you want to talk or do something," I said.

"Don't count on it, Goofy."

"What did you say?" I screamed.

"Isn't your name Goofus?" she chuckled.

"That's it. Take off my iPod and get out of my room." About that time my mom was walking by and was absolutely horrified at... me and not my evil twin.

"Abby, stop being ugly to your cousin," she screamed.

"Oh, that's okay. She didn't mean anything by it Aunt Caroline," Brooklyn lied. I was getting more confused by the minute. Brooklyn had more personalities than all of the kids in my school combined.

"Apologize, Abby."

"But Mom, she's the one being mean to me."

"Abigail!" Ooops. I know that I am getting ready to be in big trouble when my full name is called, so I quickly said that I was sorry and left my room. I was so angry that I had to call Neils.

"Neils," I began. "My cousin is a psychopath. I mean, she used to be so nice but now she is like my evil twin."

"Oh, Abby," Neils said. "She can't be that bad."

"She is and one day everyone will see her true colors," I added. Neils and I hung up the phone but not before we made plans to go to the mall in the morning with Andrea, Emily and Alison. I was thinking about a really cool purse that I wanted to buy when I heard a chuckle. Oh, no, I thought. I bet Ms. Smart-Mouth heard me say that I was going shopping.

"Shopping with the girls. I can't wait," Brooklyn sang.

"You are not invited," I yelled.

"Oh, yes I am because if I'm not invited then Aunt Caroline won't let you go."

"Great. You're invited. And Brooklyn, why are you being so mean to me?" I questioned.

"Because I don't like you. You're spoiled and a brat!" Brooklyn screamed.

I was stunned for a second time. What was that saying that Mrs. Meers taught us? Oh, yes, it now comes to mind.

"If you can't say something nice, don't say anything at all."

I finally spoke and said in a very shaky voice, "Then why do you want to go shopping with me?" I asked.

"Because I want you miserable," she said.

Oh, no, she didn't say that to me. But she had. And I was stuck to take the meanest kid to the mall with my best friends. I wanted to cry and then I wanted to scream and then I wanted to... And then she did it again.

Before dinner Brooklyn said, "Abby, I'm sorry. I don't know what's gotten into me lately. Here I pulled the chair out for you. Let's be friends again," she said sweetly. I wished later that I hadn't fallen prey to her tricks, but I had. I walked over to where the chair was and tried to sit down but since there was no chair there, I fell down on the ground. That evil kid had pulled the chair away from me and then laughed her evil head off.

"I'm going to...," I started to say, but my mom's impeccable timing stopped me.

"Time to eat, Girls. Everyone let's sit down together."

"Want me to get your chair for you?" Brooklyn giggled.

"No thanks. You've gotten the last chair that you'll ever get for me, Cruella." All I could hear was a "well" and then I heard her stomp off into the other room.

During dinner we were all sitting around

when Mom began laughing and telling everyone about the nightmare that I had involving Maria and that was the reason that I gave her to Brooklyn.

"AAAAbbby," Mom began with the story. Everyone was laughing so hard but me.

"Mom, stop it. It's not funny," I said.

"Abby, I'm sorry; you thought it was funny the other day when I was telling Grandmother Elizabeth about it. What's wrong with you today?"

"I am sorry. I guess I forgot to put on my other face like some else I know!" I screamed. The room got quiet. You know when you are getting ready to get it and that time was now. Before everyone had the chance to jump on me, I got up from the table turned around and said (nicer this time), "I am sorry. I don't think I've been feeling well," I lied. "Mom, can I take Brooklyn to the mall tomorrow with my friends."

"Well, Abigail. I will have to think on that one after that outburst. Go up to your room until I tell you to come out and then we'll see if the Abby that I know is back to planet Earth." I marched up to my room furious. I had been so happy about Brooklyn coming to my house and now I could not wait for her to go home.

What happened next was simply horrible. My dad began moving a spare bed into my room so that Brooklyn and I could spend more time together. I wanted to scream but I really wanted to go to the mall tomorrow, so I shut my mouth and said nothing.

"Double Vision"

Since Brooklyn had arrived, I had been miserable, but there was one very funny incident. My bad girl look-alike had gone outside of our house to get something out of my aunt's car when Jaxson came walking down the street. Jaxson looked over and saw Brooklyn and thought that it was me. She looked straight at Jaxson and blurted out, "What are you looking at Boy?" Jaxson's eyes bulged and he began screaming,

"Abby can see. It is a miracle. Everyone come see Abby. Abby! Look at me. How many fingers am I holding up?" Brooklyn screamed at him and said,

"I'm not Abby. I am her prettier than she is, Fatty." My mom laughed so hard and said that Jaxson just stood there looking confused.

That night my ex-favorite cousin sat down on her bed and said, "Get out of your bed and give it to me."

"Make me", I barked back. Next thing I knew she was trying to make me. She jumped on top of me and began swinging. I did what any normal girl who has a cane would do. I grabbed my cane and popped her on the head.

"AAAAgh! Abby hit me with her cane," Cruella screamed.

"Abby, what are you doing?" my mother screamed. And then luck was finally on my side. My Aunt Emma walked into the room and had seen and heard the whole bad scene.

"Brooklyn Gray! I saw everything. You apologize to your cousin, Now!"

"I'm sorry," Brooklyn said in an I-don't-really-mean-it voice.

"It's okay," I said back in an I-don't-mean-it voice back to her. My mom stepped in and said that I had had the attitude that started everything. Next thing I knew we were both grounded for the weekend and had to stay all weekend together in my room.

"Fine," I spouted. "I need a quiet weekend

where I don't have to talk to anyone." My mom and Aunt Emma shut the door on us.

I grabbed my cane and walked to the lights and turn them off because I didn't want Cruella to look at me. The lights went off and I went to sleep.

"Maria"

It was the middle of the night.

I heard, "Aaaaaby. AAAbbbyyyy. It's me again, Maria, the doll that you gave to your favorite cousin." This time it was no dream. I could really smell the paint from Maria's face and reached out and could feel her cold ceramic body. I screamed so loud that it woke up my mom, dad and my aunt. I couldn't see what happened but my Aunt Emma began screaming at Brooklyn. Obviously, Aunt Emma saw Brooklyn take Maria and place her near my face while whispering the eerie words, so that I would think that Maria was alive and would become hysterical.

"Brooklyn, how could you be so mean? You are grounded not only this weekend but next as well." She then turned to me,

"Abby, Brooklyn is having a really hard time since her dad left. She has not been her normally sweet good-natured self."

"Leave me alone," Brooklyn cried and ran into my bathroom and slammed the door. Everyone got quiet.

Even my smart mouth didn't have anything bad to say. I felt my heart sink. I mean she's really mean and hateful but I couldn't help but feel terribly sorry for her. I wanted to go into the bathroom and say something to her, but I didn't think that this was the time.

"Movie Star"

The rest of the boring weekend went off without a hitch. Brooklyn ignored me and I ignored her, but at least she wasn't pulling any of her nasty tricks on me. Mom, Emma, Brooklyn and Michael Andrew were going to shop with Grandmother Elizabeth while I got to go to school, and that sounded great to me.

That Monday morning at school, Mrs. Meers was talking to us about being role models for the kindergarten class. I love small children and couldn't wait to get my new kindergarten -reading partner, and neither could my friend, Sydney. My new friend, Sydney had moved from Rockwall, Texas to our neighborhood. She was so much fun to be around and was quickly joining our rapidly growing girl group.

Sydney had long blondish brown hair and great big blue eyes and a natural glowing tan. She has a middle school -aged brother named Brandt and yes, it is no coincidence that the jewelry store that I love named Brandt and Sydney's belongs to their parents. We couldn't wait to meet our new kindergarten pals.

My reading pal was the sweetest girl named Kelsey and Sydney's was Melissa. They were the nicest children in the class. Poor Alison had a kid named Jon who was terrible. He screamed at her when she asked him if he wanted to listen to a story about a hungry caterpillar.

"I'm hungry and I don't like caterpillars," Jon screamed.

"Great, this is going to be so much fun," Alison said sarcastically. We read with our new reading pals and then it was lunchtime.

Alison's dad, Audie had been managing our cafeteria and was doing a great job of it.

He was always so cheerful and happy until today. I instantly knew that something was wrong with him but I didn't know what.

"Hey, Audie. How's life treating you?" I joked.

"Uh, okay, Abby. How are you today?" Audie was not himself today for some reason. I heard Audie whisper to Alison as she came through the line,

"Your mother showed up at her house after you left for school today. What are we going to do?"

"Oh, no, Dad. I don't want to see her," Alison cried. What was going on? My mouth flew open again. After Alison had lied so bad about her parents being famous movie stars and then she finally came clean and told us the truth that her mother had passed away or had she been telling the truth the entire time?

Alison and I both sat quietly during lunchtime. Usually no one stops talking but today was Neils day to work her jaws while Andrea listened and gave advice.

"I don't think that Mrs. Meers likes me," Neils said.

"Why do you think that?" asked Andrea.

"Because she gave me a bad grade on my journal yesterday," Neils moaned.

"Maybe you deserved a bad grade. Neils, I saw your journal and Girl, it was sloppy." I love Andrea's directness. She says what she thinks without being rude or disrespectful to others. I wasn't paying much attention to the rest of the conversation because I was thinking about what I heard Audie say to Alison.

After lunch, I walked over to Alison and asked her right out what Audie was talking about. Alison became very quiet and then took me by the arm away from everyone else.

"Promise me you won't tell anyone?" she begged.

"I promise," I said. Then Alison told me everything. I tried not to show my surprise but it was difficulty. Come to find out, when our class first met Alison she was telling the truth. She really was the child of movie star parents and Bryce was telling the truth that he knew her and her mother Kaitlyn.

"So, Audie is not your real dad?" I asked.

"No, he isn't. Audie was my mother's cook. He felt sorry for me because my mom and dad were always gone and never had time for me. My mom bought me all kinds of wonderful things, but she left me alone. Audie was my only friend. My dad completely disappeared. Not that I missed him because I barely knew him. But I missed my mom so bad. I know that she was really young when I was born, but she didn't have the time nor was ready for a child. Eventually she told Audie to take me and to give me love and a nice home. She disappeared after that and never offered Audie a dime to help out with me."

Wow, I though. I could not believe my ears. My eyes I have never trusted but now I doubted my ears, too.

I stood there quietly and then said, "I'm sorry, Alison. You tried to tell us the truth and we wouldn't listen. We never believed you and forced you to lie. Why is your mother back now?" I asked.

"Guilt probably," Alison muttered. "She came to our house and begged to see me. I don't want to see her. I can't believe that any mother would leave her child and without any money when she has had millions to give. She just left us and never came back until now. As far as I am concerned, she can go back to old Hollywood and leave us along. Audie and I are happy and it's no thanks to her." I told Alison that I didn't blame her and that I too would be really angry. I also reminded her that her secret was safe with me.

"Alison keep me informed. I promise you

this is just between us." Alison squeezed my hand and thanked me.

"You bet I will, Abby."

That night while my evil twin was ignoring me again, I was lying in bed and thought about Alison's real mother, Kaitlyn. Kaitlyn Summers was a really well known actress. I have heard my sister Katy speak about how great her movies are. Katy once said that she wanted to be an actress just like Kaitlyn Summers and wear cool clothes like she does. Well, I thought, Kaitlyn may be a great actress but she is a sorry mother.

The next day the word had gotten out because of the newspapers and paparazzi. The paparazzi are photographers who chase down the rich and famous for pictures. Our school was buzzing and poor Alison was overwhelmed. Kaitlyn had shown up at the school and asked the secretary to see Alison. The secretary, our principal, Mrs. Cummings and the entire staff were all in a state of shock. Kaitlyn Summers' daughter attended our school along with another movie star couple's son.

Since Audie had custody of Alison and had legally adopted her, he told the office staff that Kaitlyn could not see or have any contact with Alison. I grabbed a hold of Alison by the arm and pulled her to the side.

"Alison, how do you feel? Do you want to see your mother or not?"

"Abby, I don't know how I feel right now. She left us alone and very poor. Why does she want to come back now?"

Later that night Alison called me and so did everyone else that didn't live in a cave. Katy even called and was going crazy about Kaitlyn Summers being at our school.

"Trust me," I said. "It is no big deal." When Alison called me she said that she and Audie had agreed that Kaitlyn could come by their house for a few minutes and no longer. Kaitlyn walked into their small frame house and threw her arms around Alison. Alison told me that she stood motionless and didn't know what to do so she told her mother hello and that was it.

Her mother said, "Alison, I don't blame you and Audie for hating me, but I have missed you so bad. I want to make it up to both of you."

"You're not my mother anymore. You gave me up to Audie," Alison had said. "I am very happy now and I don't want you to come here and then leave again, so go back to Hollywood and make your money."

Alison told me that Audie had not spoken a word. She said that he was scared that Alison would be taken away from him, so he just sat quietly until Kaitlyn left. Audie asked Alison how she was feeling but all Alison could say was confused. He assured Alison that if and when she wanted to see her mother that she could and that he would help her.

"Abby, Audie is a great man and I could never hurt him. I do still love my mother, but she should not have left me."

From what I heard the next few weeks, Kaitlyn left Texas and went back to California. I wished that I had known that so I could have shipped Brooklyn and Maria back with her.

"Double Bubble"

It was September and still really hot in Texas.

Other states have a cool fall in September and October but not Texans. We understand the word hot. Our fall isn't until Thanksgiving most years. Most states have the beautiful colored leaves in September, but not us. Our leaves feel like they have been fried in a pan with lots of grease.

Grandmother Elizabeth and Harry had everyone over: Mom, Dad, Katy, Michael Andrew, Cruella, I mean Brooklyn, Me, Nan and Pop for a big barbecue at their really big house with a pool similar to ours. After dinner I hung out with everyone except You-Know-Who until Harry gave us all some gum. It wasn't typical gum but gum that blew huge bubbles. I could feel the enormous swelling of my bubble when I chewed and then blew. Everyone was cracking up at all of the kids because we were blowing huge bubbles. I must have gotten too close to my mean cousin because when she blew her bubble I blew mine at the same time and the gum stuck together. I could feel Brooklyn tug one way and I tugged the other way. The gum then got tangled in our long blonde hair.

While Mom and Aunt Emma grabbed us and started pulling us apart, Brooklyn and I began laughing so hard. We giggled every time our mothers tried to pull us apart. We were completely stuck together, but it was okay because we were actually laughing and getting along for the first time since we were nine years old. I could hear Katy laughing over everyone else at the mess the gum had made.

What happened next was funny to Brooklyn and me but not to our mothers. They had to cut our long hair really short to separate us from the bubble gum.

The next day we went to a hair studio in town, and had our hair cut and styled just alike.

"Wow, Abby. We really look alike now."

After the bubble gum incident, Brooklyn was acting like the Brooklyn from the past. We spent the day together and the next. We were inseparable after that moment of the double bubble afternoon.

"Hollywood, Here She Comes"

A few weeks had gone by before Audie and Alison heard another word from Kaitlyn.

Kaitlyn called Audie and asked him if he could use any financial help with Alison. Audie politely told Kaitlyn that they were doing just fine without any help from anyone. Kaitlyn wanted to talk to Alison, so Audie put Alison on the phone.

"Hello, Allie. This is Mom, I mean Kaitlyn. Would you like to come out and spend the weekend with me? Audie can come if you would like."

Alison told me later that she didn't know what to do, so she didn't give her a definite answer. She still loved her mother but was angry with her at the same time.

Audie told Alison that if she wanted to

spend time with her mother that would be fine with him and that he would be there waiting for her to come back home. He told Alison that nothing good can come from staying angry and holding grudges, so Alison called Kaitlyn back and said that she would love to visit Hollywood again. Kaitlyn was thrilled.

The next day at school Alison was actually talking to Bryce about going back to California. He seemed so happy that Alison was once again acting like herself.

She left for California on a Thursday and took off from school on that following Friday.

She called me on Saturday night so excited that she could barely speak.

"Abby, guess who I met?" "Who?" I begged. "Hannah Montana. Can you believe it?"

"AAAAGGGGHHHH, Brooklyn come in here and listen to this," I cried.

Brooklyn came running into the room and grabbed the phone from me.

"Alison, this is Abby's cousin. Tell me what she was like?"

"She was so nice and beautiful. Tell Abby that I got her an autograph, too."

"Here, Abby. Alison has a surprise that she should tell you."

Brooklyn handed me the phone and when I heard the news I got dizzy and fainted. My once again favorite cousin helped me back up and we began screaming and laughing so loud that our mothers came into the room laughing and shaking their heads at us.

When Alison came back to school the next Monday, she told us all about her wonderful weekend. She talked nonstop about Kaitlyn.

They went to the movie studio where Alison met some of her mother's friends, they ate out at some great restaurants and went shopping.

Alison told us about all of her new great clothes, shoes and a new expensive purse. I could hear the excitement in her voice.

"I had a great time, but I missed my dad so much. I bought him his own set of pots and pans. Kaitlyn bought the best for Dad."

Even though Alison had a great time with Kaitlyn, Audie was her true parent and Kaitlyn seemed more like an older sister.

Kaitlyn once again offered to give Audie and Kaitlyn more money, Audie told Kaitlyn that it would be great for her to have a savings account for Alison's college fund. That seemed to really please Kaitlyn and she promised to call weekly and to make regular visits to see Alison.

"Audie, Alison loves you so much. I just want her to be very happy. Please let me know how and when I can help. All you two have to say is the word and I'm there."

Alison seemed a little sad when Kaitlyn left, but she was happier than she had ever been. It was true that money doesn't buy you happiness.

"Here Comes the Bride"

Katy came home from college the following weekend. She was glad to see that Brooklyn and I had become closer since our double bubble afternoon.

I noticed something different in Katy's voice. She seemed so happy and something else was up but I didn't know what.

At dinner, our whole big gang were all sitting around and talking and eating lasagna and delicious garlic bread.

Katy popped out words that I had a hard time processing, "I'm getting married."

"What?" I said.

"What?" my mom and dad said in unison.

"Before anyone gets upset I want you to know that I've been dating Rod for several months."

"Then why haven't we met him," Dad asked.

"Because, Dad, after Brewer and the other knuckleheads I wanted the next guy that I brought around my family to be the one."

Dad and Mom both got quiet, so I chimed in and said, "Are you going to share your room with him?"

"No, Abby. We are going to live near the college. He's studying to be a doctor and I want to work with children who are blind." That seemed to pep up both Mom and Dad.

"Katy, that is wonderful. I didn't know that you wanted to teach, but we need to further discuss this marriage," Mom said.

Katy seemed to ignore the last comment and began talking about teaching. Smart girl.

"I didn't know I wanted to teach until I started taking education classes. I loved the classes and want to help other children like Abby to be independent and to live a great life.

"What's your last name going to be?" I asked. "Potts," was Katy's reply.

"No, really. What's your last name going to be?"

"Abby, it is going to be Potts. I don't want

to hear any smart remarks either," Katy replied.

"Okay, Mrs. Potts," I chirped. Brooklyn and I laughed so hard and began high-fiving each other until Aunt Emma told us to settle down.

"Katy is there any way that you can keep your last name or will you be Katherine Elizabeth Diamond Butts, I mean Potts?" All the kids started laughing again.

"Mom, tell her to stop," squealed Katy.

The afternoon was strange after lunch. Mom and Dad took Katy inside of the house for a long time. I don't know what was said, but Katy left crying and angry. Mom and Aunt Emma sat up and talked late. Brooklyn and I went outside and played with my beep ball and then watched a movie.

I had a sinking feeling that Mrs. Potts was in trouble.

"Mrs. Potts"

Mom and Dad's talk must not have worked because within the next two weeks, I had a new brother-in-law and his name was Potts.

My parents were so upset at first until Mr. Potts showed up. He was really a nice guy.

I picked up on that immediately. I mean he didn't treat me any differently than any other kid just because I have a visual impairment.

Mom and Dad were equally impressed. He's going into medicine and will do his internship next fall. He was great.

Rod was great-looking with really dark black hair just like Katy's color. I could tell that Dad, Harry, Grandmother Elizabeth, Nan and Pop liked him a lot, too. I know once they meet my future husband, Brock, who is also studying to be a doctor they'll like him, too. Brock isn't aware of this yet but one day he will be.

I was really sad to see Brooklyn, Michael Andrew and Aunt Emma leave. Surprisingly enough since she had been so mean to me at first. Brooklyn had told me all of the details of her parents' divorce and they weren't pretty. No wonder she was acting badly. Anyway, the good news was that they were all getting better.

Since Brooklyn and I became close again, she was going to come back and see me next fall, and we talked on the phone every week after she left. The day she was leaving, Brooklyn carefully let Maria give me a kiss.

"Maria's going to miss you, Abby," Brooklyn said.

"I wish that I could say the same about her," I joked. We laughed, hugged and then cried because we were really going to miss each other.

"Six Flags"

The end of the school year was great. Everything seemed to work out really well. My Aunt Emma began dating a really nice man according to Brooklyn and we had a great end of the year party. The party was at Six Flags Over Texas Amusement Park. We all piled in a bus and headed off to park.

We were told to wear swimming suits under our shorts and tops because we would be riding several water rides and boy did we ever. One ride was really scary but Neils and Andrea cautioned me right before we went over this big scary hill and splashed into the water. I laughed and screamed louder than Neils and that's loud.

I was walking with my group and not to

brag, but our group is really the cool group in school when I heard someone, "Hey Abby."

"Who is it?" I asked.

"It's me Brewer. Hey tell Katy congrats on the marriage and tell her that I am the head clean-up guy at the park. Tell her that she really missed out. Too bad for her."

"I will tell her, Brewer. She'll be so mad at herself."

Andrea, Neils, Alison and I started laughing while he stood there scratching his head wondering why we were laughing.

The last day of school was our awards program.

We had to dress up and some of our parents came to see what awards if any that we were going to get.

I made the A and B Honor Roll and so did Andrea but not Neils. Not that Neils cared because she's more into sports and food like her sweet family.

The really big surprise was that they gave out an award called The Lighthouse Award for an outstanding student who had faced many obstacles and had overcome them. I bet you guessed that I won this award. Well, I didn't but Alison did. We all stood and clapped for her until our hands were crimson red.

My mom later told me that Kailtyn was there clapping and crying along with Audie.

It was such a great year, but I was getting ready for more chapters in my life and boy did I not realize how many more there would be.

"Brennan Jude"

At the end of the summer of the school year, Katy announced that she and Rod were going to have a little baby Potts.

"Hey why don't you name him Chip. Chip Potts would be great," I joked.

"Enough," my mom quipped.

"How about Sandy? Get it, Sandy Potts?" I tried again.

"Abby, one more time and you are off to your room," Mom said.

"Mom you're going to be a grandmother. What do you want to be called... Granny or Old Lady?" I was cracking myself up but not anyone else.

I heard my mom muttered to my dad,

"She's getting to be that age and acting just like Katy did."

My dad said, "Oh, I think that Abby is worse." Thanks, Guys, I wanted to scream, but I didn't because we were having a huge baby shower for Katy. It was in our huge living room because you can't have anything outside in late July in Texas or you will fry literally.

Anyway, I guessed that the baby would be a girl because the room was decorated in all shades of pink. Katy had a test that told her what the baby was going to be, so I guess it was safe to say that she was going to have a little girl. That will leave out the name Chip Potts. The shower was fantastic. There was a huge pink and white cake with pink pacifiers all over the cake. Everyone brought beautiful pink, purple, white, you name the color of baby girl outfits. Katy also received several items for a baby.

Katy and Rod had decided on a name for a little girl. Her name was going to be Peyton Caroline. Peyton Caroline was going to be my first little niece. I couldn't wait to hold and to spoil her.

The night that the baby was born was crazy. Katy and Rod caught a train before they could get to the hospital. Mom, Dad and I were following them. When it was finally time for Peyton Caroline to be born Rod came out and said,

"It's an eight pound, beautiful....boy!"

"Boy?" I questioned. " You can't name a boy Peyton Caroline, and he is going to look funny wearing all of the dresses that we have for him, too."

"What happened to the girl?" I asked.

"Abby, doctors are wrong sometimes," my mom said.

"But we have a new beautiful grandson and you have a nephew, Abby." I could feel my excitement build again. What are they going to name him," I asked.

"Clay," my mom said seriously.

"Clay Potts?" I then heard everyone burst out laughing.

"No, Abby, his name is going to be Brennan Jude. He is named after the saint of miracles," my mom said.

"He's going to need it growing up in this family," I said.

My mother took me aside and loaded another big surprise on me.

"Abby, you have a new nephew and next year, you are going to have a little brother or sister."

The next school year was really going to be interesting.

"All That Glitters"

"All that glisters is not gold;
Often have you heard that told"- Shakespeare

"Advisory"

Our school had just started a new class called Advisory. We were to meet with kids from other classes once a week and do team building activities, test taking strategies, and other cool projects. I liked Advisory class because I never know what project we are going to be doing.

Our teacher Mrs. Stone told us to get into groups of four people and build a straw tower using straw and tape. We were not to say a word but use nonverbal strategies to build our straw tower. The tallest tower that didn't topple over was the winner, and even though my group didn't win, it was really fun.

I got really excited when Mrs. Stone told us that we were going to go on a team building camp out one weekend. Everyone in our grade was going and we would all do team building activities together. Neils and I were talking about it during lunch and were really excited to go to Camp Thunderbird. Andrea and Alison were equally as excited.

I have to admit that my friends and I sit on the cool lunch table or at least we think it is cool. We like a big crowd on our table and whoever wants to join us is more than welcome. We aren't like the snoddy cool girls that you see in a movie who treat others like they are a piece of trash. In our group we think that everyone has good qualities. Yes, even old Jaxson. Jaxson and I have become really good friends the past year but when we were in the early grades, he was downright mean. He would complain about my cane or my Braille writer and want to know why I didn't go to the school for the blind. He was mean, but like I said, everyone has good qualities and Jaxson is no exception.

Jaxson sat down at the table and began complaining again about his Advisory group.

"I don't like the kids," he moaned. "They ignore me in the group and act like I don't know nothing."

"Jaxson, don't use double negatives,"

scolded Neils. "What are you talking about?" he moaned.

"When you have one negative word like no, don't, nothing, etc., the grammar rule is that you do not use two of them in the same sentence. I know your smart but you need some grammar lessons."

"I ain't sitting here today," he complained. "I'm going over and sit with Glen. He don't complain about nothing like you girls do." Poor Glen was not known for his brains but he was a nice kid.

"I heard that at Camp Thunderbird, there's bungee chord there on the camp grounds," Alison said. I couldn't wait to go and camp out a whole weekend with just my friends and okay a few teachers and chaperones. Neils, Alison, Andrea and I were so pumped about going on a camping trip with the whole grade level asked.

"Terrible Twos"

I was so excited when my nephew, Brennan Jude was born. I mean he was so tiny and was simply the best baby in the world. I would beg Katy and Rod to let me hold them, but I really didn't have to beg because they seemed to enjoy the fact that I was crazy about my little guy.

I would hold him for hours literally. Before I knew it, my precious baby wanted to crawl and then he began to pull up and then he began to take off.

My vision teacher, Ms. Ashley told me to let Brennan wear a bracelet with a bell on it so that I could hear where he was going when his little legs carried him all over the house. And boy did they ever. He ran and ran all over our house. When Brennan came over, we had to put up baby gates all over the house. Our little Potts went everywhere in spite of the baby gates. The bells would jingle like crazy. He was hilarious but I could tell that he was wearing everyone out which made me laugh even harder.

He was learning to say, "Mama and Da-da and Mine." I laughed all of the time when he was around.

One day I heard Katy say, "Mom, were we this wild? I haven't slept since he was born. I'm trying to learn Braille and trying to keep up in my Anatomy of the Eye class but he's making it impossible."

I heard Mom tell Katy that at least she was young and could keep up with him and how much my mom worried about being able to keep up with her own new baby.

"I will be forty-one-years old when my baby is born," Mom said.

"Your right, Mom. I should be thankful," Katy said. But Little Man Potts was not slowing down and making anything easier on Katy.

One day, however, I didn't think that my little guy was so funny after he got a hold of toothpaste and toilet paper.

"Mine" he shouted when Katy tried to take

the toothpaste away from him. Little Man was making my newly found sarcasm with adults seem minor. Gosh, I love that little guy.

As I have stated, one morning Little Potts was not so adorable to me. I accidentally left my brush, hairspray and flat iron on the toilet seat to pack for my camping trip with my class when I heard a splash.

"Oh, no, Brennan. Aunt Abby needs her hair supplies," I begged. All I could hear was a chuckle and more splashed.

"Brennan Jude!" I yelled. "Stop it," I scolded. I could hear his little jingle bell and tried to reach his hand to pull him out of the bathroom when that little critter grabbed my arm and bit it.

"OUCH!" I screamed. "You little...." Thankfully, I didn't finish that sentence because Nan, Pop, Mom and Katy all came rushing into the room.

"No, no, Brennan. No biting," Katy firmly stated. He obeyed his mother; there was no more biting but there was a hit from the little troublemaker and that was when he got into the doghouse.

After Katy scolded him he let out a wail that people in China could hear. You would have thought that the entire house was attacking the little guy. Finally, after one hour, he stopped crying. I turned to Mom and said,

"I can't wait for ours to get here. Yippee," I said sarcastically, three more months of freedom," and stomped out of the room.

As I was walking out of the room, I felt the sweetest and softest little arms reach around both of my knees and give me the biggest and the best hug that I had ever had. I reached down and picked up Little Potts and hugged him back, and then I couldn't wait for my Little Diamond to be born.

"The Break-Ins"

The channel 4 News was full of scary stories but nothing like the news that was going on in my neighborhood. Someone was breaking into garages and taking bicycles, expensive tools and cars. Three break-ins had already happened during the past three weeks. Andrea and I were talking about it one day at school.

"My daddy said that if anyone comes near his Mercedes, he won't wait to call the police. He said that he would chase them down himself and take them to the police station," she said.

"I wonder who would do such terrible things. I mean if you want something go to work somewhere and pay for it," I reasoned. And then of course Old Jaxson got into the gossip with us along with his new sidekick, Glen.

I think that Jaxson likes to run around with poor old Glen because it makes him feel smarter. Jaxson was blabbing away about how he would use his new karate chops on the thieves while the entire time Glen was nodding his head and agreeing with everything Jaxson was saying. Glen finally had a friend and he wasn't about to lose him.

That night at dinner, my mom and dad began talking to me about safety. They reminded me like they have several times, to lock the doors, listen and be aware of my surroundings at all times. My mom told me that she and dad were going to attend a Crime Stoppers meeting next Thursday night at Andrea's house. The Williams were heading up a Crime Watch sting for our neighborhood. In other words, we were going to look out for each other and notify the police if anything suspicious was going on.

The next Thursday night, Andrea and I played music and talked about how frightening the talk downstairs was getting to be.

"Let's go upstairs to my room and hang out," Andrea had said. We went up to her room, called Neils on the phone and just hung out.

"Hey Abby," Andrea said, "Let's go get a couple of bottles of water and some chips from downstairs. I am hungry.

"Okay. Sounds great," I replied. We walked down the stairs and could hear all of the adults yakking away about what they were going to do when they caught the robber or robbers.

"Oh, darn, Abby. We are out of water. Let's go out to the garage where our other refrigerator is. Dad bought water the other day."

We opened the door to the garage and then I heard Andrea scream.

"Who Dunnit?"

My stomach flipped over when I heard Andrea scream.

"What's wrong?" I yelled. I could hear the adults running towards the garage. My mother and Mrs. Williams were screaming,

"Are you girls, okay?"

"Yes," Andrea replied, "But our garage isn't."

My mother described to me what they were looking at. It was a mess. The robber had broken into the garage during a Crime Watch meeting and stolen Mr. Williams black Mercedes, all of his tools, and Andrea's bicycle as well as several computer games; dvd's, clothes and toys.

"I can't believe that just happened to us," Mrs. Williams cried. I felt so sorry for her and the Williams' family. I mean they were the nicest people that I had ever met.

"I saw him from the back and then got a quick look at his face," Andrea said. "He had red hair tucked up under a cap, and a scar under his right eye."

"How do you know it was him," Our neighbor, Mrs. Douglas wanted to know.

"I saw the garage door wide opened and saw a man sitting in a white van staring at me and looking into the garage. I know that it must have been him."

"We'll call the police," my mom and dad said, "Tell them everything that you saw and heard." The police came and Andrea told them exactly what she saw. They wrote down all of the information. I was still so scared that my legs were shaking.

"Mom, can we go home now?" I asked.

"Yes, Abby, as soon as the policemen are finished then we'll go home."

"Mom, can I sleep in the room with you and Dad," I asked sounding more like a four-year-old instead of mature school-aged girl.

"Sure, Abby, but don't worry. It will be fine. Everything will work out and your dad and I will both keep you safe." I hugged Andrea and told her how sorry I was that this had happened to her and to her wonderful family. She told me bye and then my parents took me home and let me sleep in their bed.

Nothing else frightening had happened in our neighborhood for a few weeks until the new neighbor moved in. He was a tall unassuming man with auburn colored hair and goatee. He looked younger than his age probably was and was attractive; however, there was a disturbing feature on his face that frightened Andrea, the scar below his right eye. He was the same person that Andrea had spotted during the robbery.

"Abby. That is the man that robbed my garage," Andrea screamed while we walked across the street from the new neighbor's house.

"Are you sure?" I asked.

"Yes, I see the scar below his right eye. I know it's him."

"Let's go tell our parents," I said. "No, net yet. No one will believe us. We need to wait and catch him in the act. One day soon, he'll mess up. We need to find the evidence when he's gone and nail him."

About the time that last word was exiting Andrea's mouth we heard the new neighbor holler at us from across the street,

"Hey Girls. My name is Richard and I'm your new neighbor. Do you live across the street from me? I wanted to ask your parents a few questions about the break-ins," Richard stated.

Andrea began to stammer, "Noo-noo," she stammered and lied. "I live on the other side of town. Come on Abby let's get home before it gets dark."

Richard yelled backed, "Well, if you girls need anything, just let me know," he answered.

"Okay, thanks, Mister, I mean Richard," Andrea sounded like a nervous cat. She later told me that Richard looked puzzled and scratched his goatee while we ran off down the street.

"Richard"

Andrea told me that her parents had met Richard and thought that he was a great guy. He told that them that he was an architect.

"What a liar," Andrea said to me.

"I know. We will get our group together and figure out what this crook is up to next, take pictures of evidence and nail him on his next break-in. In the meantime, we need to act as normal as possible around him."

"But, Abby, I told him that I didn't live here. He's going to think that I know that was him that night or he will think that I'm cuckoo," Andrea said.

"Let's go talk to him the next time that he is mowing the grass. We'll make idle talk and see if he suspects anything," I simply stated.

"Okay, but what excuses can you give him since you told him that you don't live here," I said.

"I know. Abby, I will tell him that my parents told me not to talk to strangers and that I was scared when he asked me about my parents."

"Great idea," I said. The next week we got our chance.

"Hey Richard," Andrea hollered.

"Hello," Richard answered. "I thought that you lived across town," he questioned.

"Oh, yeah, that. Well, I'm not supposed to talk to strangers," Andrea replied.

"Oh, right. Good thinking. I would like to speak more to your parents about the night the break-in happened," Richard said.

"Well. I think they are out of town or something," Andrea lied.

"Let's go Abby." Richard scratched his goatee again, shrugged his shoulders and went back to mowing the grass.

"Andrea, he is going to think that you are a troubled girl," I laughed.

"That's okay, Abby. Just as long as he stays away from my parents, he can think that I am nuts." I laughed and told her that Richard would be thinking correctly. She and I both cracked up at that one.

"Abby, one day when Richard is gone, let's go over to his garage and I will peek in and see if I see anything that belongs to my family or anyone else," Andrea said.

"Great idea, Andrea, do we want to get Neils and Alison in on this?"

"Sure, let's call ourselves The Crime Busters and have weekly meetings so that we can solve this mystery," Andrea stated.

"I will call them and fill them in on everything, Andrea," I said.

"The Secret Hideout"

The coolest thing happened to The Crime Busters' group a couple of weeks ago. Alison and Neils were adventuring through the woods when they stumbled upon an old decrepit shack that someone had abandoned. Now it was nothing to look at, but add fresh paint, flowers and other accessories and it turned into a secret hide-a-way for a crime -busting group. We decided to not tell anyone about the clubhouse, but the four of our parents and us since we were going to solve the neighborhood mystery.

I took my allowance as did Alison, Neils and Andrea and we bought lovely coats of white paint for the outside and beige paint for the inside. Andrea's mother was throwing out a really neat table with four chairs and a sofa loveseat that she gave to us. I brought pillows that Neils told me were lavender and blue. Neils brought a beautiful blue rug while Alison brought in vases of flowers, a clock, and throw blankets in case we got cold. My mom also brought us Katy's old dorm refrigerator.

The secret place was actually behind Neils's house. There were some beautiful woods behind the Roberts' home and this cottage was just across a cement wall that was at one time meant for privacy. It was our haven and a great place to solve mysteries. The really neat thing was Neils called Katy and asked her to Braille with sticky tape around the cottage for me.

The only thing that we didn't have was running water, but if we had to go to the bathroom, all we had to do was walk a few feet to the Roberts' house.

We were really impressive when we got down to business. I mean Andrea pulled out an agenda so that we were organized with how we were going to bust Richard and catch him in the act.

The first thing on the agenda was to assign positions to our group. I nominated Andrea to be president, and we all agreed.

Alison became our secretary, I was the vice president and Neils became our lookout girl. We decided that the next step would be to find out when Richard' mustang was gone and then we they would peek into the garage and see if there was anything that belonged to us. If we could prove that Richard was the same guy that stole the Williams' merchandise then we could tell our parents and then call the police. The case would be closed, and we would be the heroes.

Almost every afternoon we went to our secret cottage, and took turns bringing in sandwiches, chips, desserts and cold drinks. I loved it and couldn't wait until the end of the school day every day. It was a little like having our own place like adults do but of course we had to leave before dark.

"Camp Thunderbird"

We had to hang up our detective hats for the weekend because it was finally time for our class to go to Camp Thunderbird, and I couldn't wait to go. Even though Jaxson hated his group, I loved my group. They were really cool kids.

I loved hanging out with Whitney. Whitney the group said was a true beauty with outstanding blue/green eyes, naturally dark skin and long brownish/blonde hair. The other kids were Blake, Emily and Shelby. Emily was very pretty with long brown hair and large hazel eyes. She was tiny and had really long eyelashes. Shelby and Blake were actually brother and sister both with great-looking dark curly hair and big green eyes.

We had the best time doing our group

projects. We laughed and got along really well. Jaxson wasn't so lucky with his group but at least he had Glen to hang out with. As I have said in the past Glen wasn't known for his brains but he was really a nice kid.

Our parents all drove us to the school where we would board our school bus and have a great weekend together at Camp Thunderbird. My mom always gets a little weepy anytime I go off even for a weekend. Dad is hilarious. He throws my suitcase on the bus, says bye to me, jumps in the car and starts to idle it to let my mom know that he is in a hurry whether he really is or not. So, after our good-bys to our families, we boarded the bus and took off for an adventure that was going to be more than we bargained for. The great news was that we got to pick our own cabin mates, so The Four Musketeers got to camp together.

Our cabin was called "The Eagle". We took our bags, unpacked and sat around until dinner. After dinner we were to meet with our group outside around a huge bonfire. We sang songs, saw or in my case heard a corny skit put on by our teachers and then met with our individual advisory groups. My group met by a huge oak tree. My friend Emily told me all about the area. We took a brief walk while she explained my surroundings to me.

"Look, Abby. Take your hands and feel of this tall oak," Emily had explained. She was really cool. Whitney came up and took my arm while we walked over to where the group was meeting. Blake was hilarious. He said,

"Normally I would complain about being the only male in the group but not this time." We laughed at everything he said. Why do girls laugh and giggle when a guy is around? Guys punch, tackle or act cool but girls just laugh like hyenas.

The counselors came around and met with us. Our counselor was a really funny lady named Karen. Karen had beautiful red hair. She reminded us that we were to meet together and teach the others in our group something that we know well. We had already discussed this in our groups at school, so I felt prepared to teach my lesson.

In my backpack I brought blindfolds so that the kids could do an activity under blindfold and see what it was really like to not be able to see.

We passed around the blindfolds while Karen laughed along with us. The kids put the blindfolds on, each took a paper cup and tried to pour water from a pitcher of water that Karen was taking from person to person. I could hear the water splashing and kids laughing really hard.

"It's not so easy is it?" I questioned.

"No, Abby, it isn't," they all answered in unison. Next it was Emily's turn. Emily is really great at making delicious desserts. She gave us marshmallows, a bar of chocolate and graham crackers. We roasted the marshmallow over the small campfire and placed the chocolate and hot marshmallow between two graham crackers. It was delicious.

"Emily, will you teach me how to cook?" I asked.

"Yes, Abby. Why don't you come over after school one day and we will cook with my mom who also happens to be a great cook."

Blake asked us all to get up and watch him kick a soccer ball really far. We took turns kicking the ball. He was so nice and patient with me. He took my hands and said,

"Abby feel of the ball down here." I did what he said and then he gently showed me how to kick the ball hard. He positioned my leg behind me and then told me to bring it forward really quick.

"Way to go Abby," Blake cheered. I could feel my face blush. "Thanks, Blake. I didn't do too badly but I don't think that I'm ready for a position on the Cowboys, yet." Blake and Whitney cracked up laughing and then Whitney showed us how to do flips.

I could hear her flipping all over the place. I attempted a clumsy cartwheel and fell in the dirt. Shelby and I laughed and laughed.

"Abby are you okay?" asked Karen.

"Great," I said, "never better." Shelby's activity was really cool, too. We learned how to make stitches with yarn and a crochet needle. I could feel the places where I needed to go in and out of.

"Tricks"

It was truly a great time. The night in the cabin The Four Musketeers were chatting, laughing and playing tricks on each other. For example, some funny red head put crackers on my pillow.

"I'll get you yet, Neils," I joked.

"Come and get me, Abby Diamond," Neils laughed. I waited and planned my retaliation with Alison's help. We got Neils's cell phone and told her that her mother was on the phone. When Neils picked up the phone and placed it to her ear, she found shaving cream on the listening part. She found it all right. It was in her hair. We must have really been getting loud because we heard a knock on the door and then a loud,

"Keep it down, Girls. Hiking all day tomorrow. Rest up," Karen had said.

"Okay. Night, Karen," we all said. "Good night," Karen replied. Of course, we didn't go to sleep until really late, but we tried not to let anyone hear us.

"Lost"

The next morning we were all really tired at breakfast but felt great because we were going on an adventure. Our camp director was Fran. She told us the rules before we began our nature hike. We were all placed with our advisory group and given a color. I was in the red group and Glen and Jaxson were the yellow group.

"Okay. Listen up," Fran began.

"Everyone look for your color ribbons that will be tied to the trees. When you see a ribbon you will also see a number on the tree. Take the ribbon off of the tree and place it in your paper sack. The first group to return back to camp will be the winner of the trophy. We will have a second and third place winner as well."

Every group had a college student walking with them. The hike was to take approximately three to four hours because we would stop, rest and eat our lunch from our backpack. We were told that cell phones did not work in the woods unfortunately but that we would be safe traveling with our young adult and group. My group had one extra kid, Emily who was to give me extra help if I needed it, but no one thought that I would need much help.

We got to meet our ditz, oops, I mean our college student. Her name was Chrissy and as soon as I met her I wondered if she and Brewer had been separated at birth. I mean they are both so, well, not the sharpest pencil in the box.

"Hey Y'all," Chrissy said with a drawn out Texas accent.

"Let's get started. Which way do we go?" she asked me.

"I'm blind and you're suppose to be the adult."

"Oh, yes, you are right, Abby," Chrissy said.

Oh brother, I thought. If my mom had met Chrissy before this camping trip I would be at home babysitting Brennan.

"Come on, Abby. I'll take care of you," said Blake. "Thanks, Blake. I don't have too much confidence in our fearless leader," I said.

"I don't either," Blake cried. "Well, at least I'm good in the outdoors."

We all walked for two hours and the weather, smells and sounds were wonderful. It was great to be in the outdoors, smell the air and hear the sounds of the animals. We all found a rock, sat around and ate our lunch. We had already found the eighth ribbon out of ten. After we had found the tenth ribbon we were then to find the next ten ribbons back to the main campground.

"Abby, I'm getting scared," Neils told me. "Why, Neils? What is wrong?" I asked. The past couple of months her belief in herself had taken a nosedive for unknown reasons.

"Don't worry, Neils. This is really fun. We'll be heading back soon." Just then we noticed that Ms. Bubblehead was missing.

"Where is Chrissy?" Emily asked. We all got up and started searching for Chrissy. She had simply disappeared. I then heard someone talking. It wasn't Chrissy though, it was Jaxson, Glen and their group. I could hear some girls griping at Jaxson and Glen.

"You boys better get us out of this mess," some smart-mouthed girl said.

"Why don't you Ms. Know-It-All," Jaxson retorted. "Yeah" was all Glen said back. said back.

"Jaxson what is going on?" asked Blake.

"Well, it seems that your group's leader and my group's leader wanted to go exploring and they left us here by ourselves. They both also forgot to show us how to get back because they didn't finish placing ribbons on the trees," Jaxson screamed.

"Oh, no," Neils screamed.

"Neils, calm down," Whitney said. "We'll find our way back." But we didn't. At least not for another four hours. It started getting dark and our two groups were getting more and more lost.

"Surely, someone is looking for us," Emily said.

"Abby, watch out," I heard Glen say.

"The plant that you are about to step on has three points, so it is Poison Ivy."

"Thanks, Glen," I said surprised. Glen was not known for his brains after all. Later when we were all starving, Glen found us berries that were great to eat and not harmful.

"How do you know that this won't kill us," asked Jaxson.

"Because," Glen began, "My Boy Scout group comes out here a lot. I ain't good in school but I love the outdoors." I was surprised and happy for Glen. He and Neils began talking and came up with a great idea.

"Hey Everyone. Listen up. Glen and I have an idea. Get into partners. One partner will put on the blindfolds that Abby brought and lead the other partner through the dark woods. The reason for that is that our vision is getting in the way of finding our way back. Some people keep thinking that they "see" the way out and it is only getting more confusing, so we are going to be like Abby and use our other senses to get back to the campgrounds." Neils and Glen were geniuses. Their plan actually worked.

Emily said, "I hear the bubbling creek. I heard that sound on the way up here."

"Great," said Glen, "and I remember this broken tree branch that I just about broke my neck on," he said.

"I can smell the strong damp smell of dirt that I had smelled earlier," I chimed in. Before we knew it we had finally made it back to camp. Everyone, especially Karen and Fran were thrilled to see us. Kids and adults began hugging and complimenting us on acting like adults.

"Red and Yellow groups, don't worry. You're college helpers will never help us again at Camp Thunderbird. They have been fired for being so irresponsible," Fran said.

"Hey, Fran," I said. "We don't need them anyway. All we need is two intelligent people like Neils and Glen," I said. Everybody started clapping. I could hear the old Neils's funny laugh return and so did her confidence.

"All that Glitters"

My mom has told me the saying, "All that glitters is not gold."

"What does that mean?" I had asked.

"It means that people assume certain things that aren't correct. For example, someone may think that they have found gold in the dirt but it's not gold; it's a piece of glitter. It looked like gold, it sparkled like gold, but when you closely examine it, it isn't gold it's a piece of glitter," my mom had explained. That comes to my mind when I think back to the weekend after the camping trip.

Speaking of my mom, I accidentally bumped into her when we had been preparing dinner when I noticed the big bump that was now her stomach.

"Wow, Mom. When is our little guy going to get here?" I asked.

"Soon, Abby, but it isn't going to be soon enough for me," she added.

Mom sounded so tired and a little grouchy these days, but back to keeping her wise words in the back of my mind, The Four Musketeers met at the hide-away and began making plans to spy or snoop.

We met and Andrea began our meeting while Alison and I made everyone a sandwich.

Neils' mom also brought us a hot batch of chocolate chips cookies and freshly squeezed lemonade to drink.

"Today is the day," Andrea began. "Richard is leaving today to go on a business trip around three o'clock this afternoon. We'll watch him from my garage window and then when he leaves, we're going to go peek into all of the windows."

"How do you know what time he is leaving?" I asked.

"Because he told my parents that after he went snooping again to see what they knew about the break-ins." Around 3:00 that day, Richard the Crook was leaving at exactly 3:00. He pulled out of the driveway with his loaded down truck that happened to be covered by a blue tarp.

"Hmmm," Alison said. "Why do you need to cover something legal with a tarp?"

"Great question," Andrea said. "Let's go and find out."

We ran across the street and began our unofficial police work. I cupped my hands as did Neils, so that Andrea and Alison could be boosted up to see into the garage windows. "Oh, my gosh!" Alison had gasped.

"Crazy Girls"

"What's going on?" I yelled. "Tell us what you see!"

"Abby, Neils, I see my bicycle and some of dad's tools all broken into pieces. I'm going to squeal on that creep today and hope he goes to jail tonight." About that time, I could hear the sound of tires driving up the driveway. It was Richard and he was back.

"What are you girls doing?" he yelled. We took off running and ran fast. Andrea grabbed me by hand and our feet flew as fast as track runners' feet.

"I'm going to talk to your parents about this," Richard yelled.

"Great," said Andrea, " I'm going to call the police because you're the crook in the neighborhood. I saw you that night and I

have seen the stolen goods in your garage."
I could have fainted when I heard Andrea
going off. She was mad, I mean realllllly
mad. I almost felt sorry for Richard.

The next thing that happened totally
caught me off guard. Richard was following
us. He was running across the street after
us.

"Hurry," Neils yelled. "He's going to kill
us."

"What are you talking about?" Richard
questioned.

"Kids in my neighborhood aren't this crazy.
I may not live in Dallywood like you kids, but
at least our kids act normally."

Mr. Williams heard the commotion and
came outside.

"Hey Richard. Is something wrong?"

"Daddy, don't listen to him. He has all of
the stolen goods from his neighborhood and
stored them in his garage."

To our surprise, Mr. Williams and Richard
both began laughing so hard at us.

"What's so funny?" Andrea screamed.

"Can all of you keep a secret?" Mr. Williams
asked.

"Yes," I spoke for everyone.

"Richard is an undercover policeman.

He's been investigating the robberies and is on to someone that's been robbing the neighborhoods around here. The man takes parts off of merchandise and sells them. He then dumps the parts all over the junkyard. That is what you're seeing. The policemen are using the house across the street as a headquarters."

"Now, please keep quiet about all of this because we are going to arrest the man today," Richard asked.

"We will," we all promised.

"Well, just out of curiosity, what was underneath the blue tarp that you were driving off with," I asked.

"All of those items had the crook's fingerprints actually on the items. I was on my way to take the item back to the police station," Richard explained.

"Wait here. I'm going to bring something back to you." We waited with Mr. Roberts and wandered what was inside that Richard was bringing to us.

"I speak regularly to schools and pass out my cards, fake police badges and safety rules. Please take them and if you ever need anything, don't hesitate to call me."

"What about Abby's card?" Mr. Roberts asked.

"Her card needs to be in Braille so that she can have the number, too."

"Thanks, Mr. Roberts, but I'll take mine home, ask my mom to read the information for me and then I'll put everything into my note taker."

"Well," said Mr. Roberts. "Sometimes things aren't what they seem." And then to my friends' surprise I quoted my mother's quote, "Yes, Mr. Roberts. All that glitters is not gold."

"Chip Off the Ol' Block"

I bet you're thinking that something crazy must have happened the day that my baby brother was born. Well, surprisingly enough, it was a calm day.

My dad simply took my mother to the hospital and three hours later I had a new baby brother named Kaleb Chambers Diamond. Chambers is a family name, so my mom stuck that in the middle of his name. I held him only hours after he was born. I was so proud to hold my own little brother. He was simply perfect. My mom told me that he looked exactly like my dad. I laughed and said, "He's a chip off the old diamond, I mean block." We laughed and the next thing that I knew our new baby's nickname was Chip.

Mom and Dad had turned Katy's old room

into a beautiful baby nursery decorated in a Noah's Ark theme. Mom asked Aunt Blake to paint a beautiful water scene on the wall with a boat filled with two of every animal and an old man in a robe who was suppose to be Noah. Chip had several stuffed animals, a blue crib and a nice soft rug that went along with the theme of the room.

I loved Chip so much unless it was 1:00 am. He had some sort of built in timer that went off every night. "WAAAAAA-WAAAAAAAA", every morning at 1:00. I loved that little guy every minute of every day except for that time of the morning. Of course I quickly forgot about my irritation when I get my nightly wake up call because I get to feed and hold the smallest diamond.

"California"

We were going to California and visit my Aunt Emma, Michael Andrew and my favorite cousin, Brooklyn since we had a fall break that was going to last a couple of weeks. I couldn't wait to see Brooklyn. We had been talking frequently the past several months on the telephone, emailed weekly and sent each other pictures.

When we arrived in California, Brooklyn thought that Chip was adorable and he was. After our flight, Brooklyn, Aunt Emma and Michael Andrew had picked us up from the airport and taken us back to their house. They had a great house in Los Angeles. It was really large and had a nice pool in the backyard. Brooklyn had a king-sized bed, so I got to stay in her room with her.

We stayed up late one night laughing and talking. We even joked about Maria, the doll that I had given to her. I was relieved, however, when she told me that Maria was safely resting in the closet.

"Abby, I have missed you so much," Brooklyn had said.

"I have missed you, too. Let's just the two of us go shopping at the mall tomorrow."

"That sounds great. Today Mom wants all of us to go to the beach, so we can hang out with everyone today and then go off on our own tomorrow."

The next day was a blast. We went to the beach and played in the sand. We ate hotdogs, coconut snow cones, and candy at the beach. We swam with our inner tubes and floaties while Mom and Aunt Emma sat underneath a tent where it was breezy and cool with Baby Chip. We laughed really hard when Brooklyn let Michael Andrew and me bury her in the sand with our buckets. That night after the fun in the sun we went straight to bed and dozed off.

"The Little Star"

The next day Brooklyn and I couldn't wait to go shopping. We are both like Nan, even though Nan is my dad's mother. We shop 'til we drop.

Mom and Aunt Emma agreed to let us go shopping at the mall near their home. She gave me a limit that I could spend on her credit card as did Aunt Emma with Brooklyn. After we shopped and bought some really cool clothes and shoes, we sat down at the Food Court and ate some delicious tacos. I could hear a cheer downstairs.

"Someone famous must be here to sing," Brooklyn said.

"How do you know?" I asked. "Well, there's a huge crowd down below. I can see cameras flashing and security guards."

A few minutes later I heard someone announce a song and then the most beautiful song was sung by the most outstanding voice that I had ever heard.

"Wow. That kid can sure sing," I said to Brooklyn.

"Abby, guess what? There's a movie star down below listening to her kid sing. I now understand why there are so many cameras going off. I wonder who it is?" Brooklyn asked.

"It's Kaitlyn Summers. She's here to listen to her daughter sing," a young girl told us.

I dropped my taco.

The Lost Treasure

There is a place where the sidewalk ends
And before the street begins,
And there the grass grows soft and white,
And there the sun burns crimson bright,
And there the moon-bird rests from his flight
To cool in the peppermint wind.

Adventures of
Abby Diamond

Let us leave this place where the smoke blows black
And the dark street winds and bends.
Past the pits where the asphalt flowers grow
We shall walk with a walk that is measured and slow,
And watch where the chalk-white arrows go
To the place where the sidewalk ends.

Yes we'll walk with a walk that is measured and slow,
And we'll go where the chalk-white arrows go,
For the children, they mark, and the children, they know
The place where the sidewalk ends.

By: Shel Silverstein

"The Last Day"

It was the last day of school and boy were we living it up. The Four Musketeers were listening to music and eating cookies during gym time.

Coach Smith our PE coach was really cool about that type of thing. As long as we are doing what we are supposed to be doing, he'd let us eat before the holidays or on the last day of school.

"Hey Alison, are you going to California this summer and stay with your mom?" Andrea asked.

"No, my mom is doing a movie in Europe, so Audie and I are going to hang out and have what he calls a Stay Vacation. In other words, we will just do things around our neighborhood," Alison replied.

"Hey Everyone. My Grand Pop and Nan are taking me to Galveston to a really neat water park. We are going to hang out all weekend. I have already asked them if I could bring my bestest friends and they said yes. My Grandmother Elizabeth said that she would pay for all of us to go and have a really great time."

"I am in," squealed Neils. "I am ready for a girls' weekend and ready to get away from my three brothers."

"I can go, too," Andrea cheered. "My mom is already ready for me to find things to do," Andrea laughed.

"We are going to have the best time in Galveston. I can't wait. As you know, my Nan and Grand Pop are the coolest. They are going to take us to the water park, on tours and anything else that we want to do." Just as I was finishing my last sentence, Old Jaxson and Glen walked up.

"Water Park sounds great to me," he said.

"Me, too," echoed the Parrot.

"Neither one of you are invited," Neils told them.

"Sorry, Boys, girls only on this trip," I said.

"I don't need you girls to have fun," said Jaxson. "I have a slide that I get wet and slide on." "Great, have fun and don't break a leg," Alison laughed.

The bell rang and we went into our classroom. Everyone feels so free to do whatever on the last day of school. We were helping Mrs. Johnson clean up the room, so that we could get ready for the party. Kids were laughing and getting a little rowdy when I heard the sweet Mrs. Johnson scream, and I mean scream, "SIT DOWN IN YOUR CHAIRS, NOW!" The whole class scrambled to get back to their seat. I was a little disoriented and politely said in a tiny voice,

"I don't know where I am." That seemed to break the ice for whatever reason because Mrs. Johnson then burst into laughter.

"Oh, Abby. You won't let me stay mad, will you?" The class laughed too but seemed to settle down before our class party. My mom couldn't be there because she was doing her own class party, but Andrea's mother, Mrs. Williams and Glen's mother were there. The funny thing is that Glen's mother is exactly like Glen. Anything Mrs. Williams would say, the senior parrot would echo. It was hilarious.

After what seemed like a really long day of cookies, cokes, pizzas and videos, the bell to summer freedom finally rang. We all ran out cheering, laughing, clapping and did whatever else we felt to express the overwhelming feeling of total freedom. That night I packed my bags for a vacation that I could never forget.

"Galveston"

The next morning Neils, Andrea and Alison's parents dropped them off at my house a few minutes before Grand Pop and Nan picked us up.

"Now girls. I know that you are all great kids, but I do not want you giving Pop and Nan any grief.

Abby, that means for once not solving mysteries. Just go on the trip and enjoy yourselves. Galveston has always been one of my favorite places to vacation."

"We'll be so great, Mrs. Diamond. We will mind all of our P's and Q's, " said Neils.

"Great Neils. I'll put you in charge of making sure that there are no mysteries to solve. Just a fun and relaxing vacation."

"You got it, Mrs. D."

Just about that time Grand Pop and Nan drove up in their rented SUV, so that we would all have plenty of room. It came with a DVD player. Nan had already called and told me to bring along some favorite movies.

They had coolers packed to the gills, cookies, chips and anything else that makes you fat and is not good for you. Like I've said before, I love these people. So, we were on our way to Galveston, Texas, all of The Four Musketeers listening and watching our favorite movies. We didn't realize that another adventure was just around the corner.

"Quack, Quack"

We were staying at a really cool motel near the Water Park. Nan and Pop got two adjoining rooms, so we felt like we were in our own apartment.

"I love getting older," Neils beamed. "I can't wait until we all go off to college, live together and become police women together. We'll solve all types of crime."

"I'm with you," I added.

"Me, too," said Alison. "I have seen a little taste of fame after my mom had me singing at different malls and with that dumb manager. I don't want any part of the flashy life again. It just isn't worth it," she said.

"I want to be the medical examiner," Andrea added. "We can all solve mysteries and fight crime together. We can call our group, 'Blind Justice' or something catchy like that." We all cracked up but became really serious about going into crime busting for a living.

"Abby, y'all get ready. Grand Pop and I are going to take y'all on a tour that you'll love. It's called the Duck Tours. The bus travels around Galveston and talks about the history and then the bus turns into a boat and is actually in the shape of a duck.

"We'll go into the bay and float on the water," Nan beamed.

"YES!" Neils shouted. "Hey, Nan?" Neils continued,

"Can we also play miniature golf along Stewart Beach?" All of my buddies call my grandparents what I call them. I just love the closeness.

"You bet, Neils. But I have to warn you, I play eighteen holes of golf every week." Nan wasn't kidding either. We all played miniature golf on the seawall and she beat the pants off of us. I mean she slaughtered us and then won a free pass at the end.

"Boy, Abby. I hope that I can play golf that well when I'm sixteen let alone sixty," Andrea said.

The golf place was really cute. While you

were putting the golf ball around you could hear the beautiful sounds of the ocean waves and smell the salty air.

"Okay. Let's go on the Duck Tour bus," Grand Pop announced. We all got on the bus. The tour was fascinating. The driver told us all about the history of Galveston and how some think that Jean Lafitte, the pirate's hidden treasure might be on the island somewhere. According to the tour guide, Jean Lafitte was friends with Napoleon and helped him to escape France and hid his treasure for him.

"Wow," Neils said. "I wish I was a pirate."

"No way, Neils, you won't get your ears pierced, so you'll have to think of another career," Andrea laughed and so did we. Nan and the tour guide announced that the bus was about to be turned into a boat. I heard the splash and into the water we went. It was so cool. The tour guide continued to tell us that during World War II the bus/boats were used to transport our service people. It was time to leave the water when the whole tour became laughing really hard.

"What's going on?" I asked Alison.

"Oh, Abby the birds won't get out of the way. A really old lady just walked down, grabbed the birds by the bills and tossed them back into the water. She's hilarious. She has really short gray hair, wearing shorts that are way too short, a tank top and no shoes and a great smile." Everyone began clapping for the lady. She smiled and waved us off. After the tour, we walked in and out of souvenir shops.

As I've said before Nan is a "Shop 'Til You Drop' woman. This is another reason that she is one of my favorite people on the planet. We bought all types of fun souvenirs. I got a really cool necklace, an ankle bracelet, and a t-shirt. Neils was telling me that she bought a t-shirt and a pirate hat so that she could be like Jean Lafitte. She always cracks me up. Alison and Andrea bought hats, necklaces, t-shirts and water bottles. We were having the best time. We just didn't realize what was going to happen next.

"The Water Park"

We were all so tired that after all of the fun we immediately went straight to bed. The next morning I couldn't wait to get to the Water Park.

"Come on, Abby. Get up," yelled Andrea.

"Okay, let me find my bathing suit and swimsuit cover-up, grab my flip-flops and I 'm ready," I squealed.

"Don't forget your towel and sunscreen," reminded Alison. About that time Nan came into our room loaded down with two ice chest, cookies and other snacks.

"Your Grand Pop is going fishing, so while you girls are riding those scary water rides I'll be in our own private cabana. Abby, I will give you landmarks in case you get separated. Remember Andrea you and Abby are to ride in a double float when riding the fast rapids at the Water Park." "

You bet, Nana," Andrea replied. "I'll watch this crazy girl like a hawk."

"I know you will and that's why I selected you. All of you girls are so good to help Abby out and I appreciate it so much," Nana said.

"She helps us out, too, Nana," laughed Neils. Since we stayed right across the street from the Water Park we were there within a matter of five minutes.

"Look," said Alison, "They are letting everyone go in." We walked in and found the landmarks that I needed and then put all of our junk down inside of Cabana #16. We got the end one that was placed right beside the lifeguard, so it was nice and quiet for Nana.

We all grabbed our inner tubes; Andrea and I in our double one, got in the water and rode down a cool tunnel into some roaring rapids. "AAAAAAGGGGGHHHHHHH!!!!" screamed Neils but only to make us laugh because Neils was not scared of anyone or anything. It was a blast. We rode up a conveyer belt and then drop into more roaring rapids. We then walked up several stairs and rode a really twisted ride. I screamed but not because I was trying to make people laugh. I was scared!

"Abbbbbbbyyyyyyyyyyy. Arrrreeeee yooooouuuuu oooooookaaaayyyy?" echoed Andrea.

"Yes, I think so," was all that I could let out. After the ride we were all laughing so hard about my loud scream.

"Hey I could hear you from all of the way down here," said an unknown voice.

"Who are you?" I asked. "Hi. My name is Campbell. Since I am in a wheelchair I can't go down the slides but I get a kick out of listening to people scream on the slides," Campbell chuckled. We sat and talked to Campbell after introducing ourselves. He told us that he was exactly our age and lived with his grandmother on the island. What was really weird was that she was the woman who got rid of the birds for us when we took the Duck Tour Campbell told us.

"She loves that tour bus. She listens for it, and goes out and helps the driver if the ducks or birds get in the way. She's great plus it gives her something to do." Campbell was a really cool guy. We sat around and talked and told him about how we loved to solve mysteries.

"Hey Abby. Here's your bag from Nana," Neils said.

"She told us that she put some money in your bag, so that we could go and get some grub to eat."

We told Campbell good-by and went and bought twelve hot dogs, five bags of chips and sodas even though Nan had some of that already packed. We ate, waited our usual thirty minutes so that we would not get stomach cramps and took off to ride more fun rides. We met up with a cool group of kids from Austin, Texas who were at the Water Park on a church trip. One girl was really cool. Her name was Kamryn. She and I rode the Lazy River a few times together.

After we hung out with the kids from the church group for a while, we were all so tired and ready to leave.

We left the Water Park during the late afternoon so that we could get ready for dinner, more miniature golf and whatever else we decided to do.

After we got back to the hotel a really strange thing happened. A cell phone rang that did not belong to me was ringing from my new beach bag that Nana bought last night.

"Hello," I answered.

"Please help me," the unknown child voice began. "I need for you to find the treasure that belongs to my relatives. I know that you and your best friends solve mysteries. Please help. I will call again later." The unknown caller then abruptly hung up.

"What was that all about, Abby?" Andrea asked. "And I didn't know that you had two cell phones."

"I don't," I added. "Someone put a cell phone in my bag and then called to ask me if we would all find the hidden treasure that belonged to his/her relatives.

"Well, if I look for another hidden treasure, I ain't giving it up," Neils laughed.

"Hey Neils," Alison said, "You and Jaxson are becoming too good of friends and sounding more and more alike." They laughed and then Neils got serious.

"Really, Abby. Who had time to put a cell phone into your bag? And why can't they find the treasure themselves? You don't think it's your dad again trying to teach us another life lesson, do you," Neils asked.

"No, it was the voice of a kid around our

age but I couldn't tell if it was a girl or a boy because they muffled their voice."

"You better not tell Nana," Neils warned, "Because if you do she'll tell your mother that you are trying to solve another mystery and then you'll be in big trouble."

"Oh, yeah, that's right. Okay no one say a wordand we'll see what happens next with the cell phone. Who knows maybe it's just a prank," I said in an uncertain way.

"Sure, Abby. Cell phones just drop into our bags on a daily basis," Andrea joked.

"I know," I said. "I just wish that Mom hadn't told me to stay away from mysteries on this trip."

"More Clues"

We ate at The Rainforest Café and it was wonderful. Neils described everything that she was seeing to me. She took my hands and let me feel of a huge hairy toy snake.

"Gross," I squealed. Neils began laughing. After dinner when we were getting ready to leave my mysterious cell phone rang. I grabbed before Nana recognized that it was not really my phone.

"Hello," I said in a casual tone.

"I need your help," the voice whispered.

"What do you want me to do?" I asked. "The clues to the map are found in different parts of Galveston. And only I know where that is. Go to the east end of the beach where you will see a large hotel. Look underneath the first bench that you come to. It's engraved and says, 'For Jane'. That's all for now." And then the scary rascal hung up.

"Who are you talking to?" asked Nana.

"My friend from School from the Blind," I lied. Oh, no. Every time I lie there are always consequences but I really wanted to help for some reason. There seemed to be such desperation in the kid's voice.

"Abby," Neils reasoned. "You are going to be in big trouble. Your mom said no mysteries and I told her that I would help you to avoid them."

"I know, Neils," I said. "But this kid really needs us." "Why doesn't he or she go and get the maps himself?" Neils questioned.

"Great thought. I'll ask the next time that the person calls," I answered.

After Nana clobbered us in three games of miniature golf, I heard a man saying, "I shot a hole-in-one. Why didn't the buzzer go off?" His wife and children were laughing really hard behind his back Alison said.

"Hey Nana. Can we go and see that really large hotel on the beach?" I asked.

"Sure Abby. Let's go," Nana replied. "What are you doing?" Andrea whispered to me.

"We are going to get into big trouble."

Neil's' shoulders and pull it down. I distracted Nan by asking her to explain what the word 'par' meant. She eagerly agreed.

"Abby each hold has a par. For example, if the par says two then you should make the hole in two tries." I heard the group giggling and clapping, so I knew that they had the map.

"What are you girls yelping about?" laughed Nan.

"Nan, you wouldn't believe us if we told you," joked Neils.

"Probably not. Let's move so that I can score more holes-in-one," teased Nan. The phone in my bag began ringing.

"Hello," I whispered. The voice said,

"Great work. You have the map. The next clue is for you and your friends to go where the bishop scores a checkmate. Things will really heat up under the star." I heard a loud click in my ear. I told the gang about the clue.

"Hmmm," Andrea thought. "This clue will definitely take some time to figure out." Later that night we went swimming in the hotel pool. It was really cool. It had a swim-up bar, so you could order your soft drinks while you swam. We ordered our soft drinks and then swam back over to the side of the pool.

"I wonder if the kid is talking about the king-sized chess set in the middle of The Strand. Remember where the cool kids were spray painting beautiful sunset pictures," Alison pondered.

"Great thought," Andrea said and then added excitedly, "Remember when Nan and Pop told us about the really smart lawyer, Walter Grisham who built a huge house before the terrible hurricane of the 1900's that literally blew away the island but not the house that he built?"

"Yes," Neils said. "He helped hundreds of people that were homeless by letting them stay in their really large house. After he passed away, his wife sold it to the diocese and the bishop moved into it. That has to be what this clue is all about." Neils and Andrea, I had a feeling, were exactly right. I asked Nan and Pop to take us to the Bishop's Palace. They agreed but we first spend a day of fun in the sun.

"The Tide is High"

The following morning the gang, Nan and Pop and I went to a buffet after we changed into our bathing suits and of course our cover-ups and flip-flops. We had a delicious breakfast at the hotel that was all you can eat buffet.

"Neils, I love a girl with a hearty appetite," Grand Pop laughed. We ate scrambled eggs, buttered toast, and bacon and then we all split a huge cinnamon roll with more icing than you have ever seen. We were full after breakfast so first we strolled around the souvenir shops while Grand Pop went down on the beach and rented us our own umbrella and chairs. We bought more treasures that we couldn't live without like seashells, more t-shirts, sand buckets and another boogie board, and then we met Grand Pop on the beach.

I loved getting out into the waves on my boogie board. Since Neils is the most athletic one, she rode on my board with me. We were having the best time even though I hated when I swallowed a huge amount of salt water after riding a really big wave. Yuck. After I was worn out Alison told me that Neils and Andrea were actually surfing on their boards.

"You go, Girls," I screamed loudly. While the more athletic ones were riding the waves, Alison and I build more sand castles. We simply dumped out the buckets filled with sand, made a moat to go around our castles and even made some really cool windows. Pop walked across the street and bought us some great hamburgers and fries. We had our ice chest full of drinks and snacks.

"Wow, look at Abby," Andrea said. "Abby you have got a tan as dark as Sydney's."

"What does that mean exactly?" I asked.

"Well," Andrea said, "Your skin was the color of a marshmallow and now it's the color of a caramel."

"Oh, goody. I love caramels."

The coolest thing happened next. A dark haired man with really blue eyes was asking a beautiful dark haired woman to marry him. A lady next to us told us that his name was Scott and her name Claire. Scott had hidden the engagement ring into a seashell and pulled it out in front of her. While we were all 'oooing, and ahhhing,' as Scott and Claire were celebrating, Neils went back to surfing on the waves. Alison and I began hunting for seashells just like the couple was. We found some great ones and placed them into Alison's new red backpack that she had just purchased.

After we left the beach we changed into our shorts and got headed to the Bishop's Palace.

"Treasure Hunt"

"I'm so glad that you girls are into learning some history. I have to admit that when I was your age I was only interested in shopping," Nan said.

"You haven't changed much you Shop Girl," I laughed.

"So Nan, what is the Bishop's Palace and why is it such a great place to visit?" asked Neils.

"Well, you see, during the 1800's Galveston was where the really wealthy people lived. A really smart lawyer named Walter Grisham and his wife had this spectacular home built. He didn't inherit his money but made it on his own penny by penny. The home is gorgeous. However during the hurricane of 1900 the entire island was wiped away. It was similar to what happened to New Orleans during the horrible hurricane Katrina.

According to historians, it was as if God took His hand and wiped away the entire island over night. Many people were left homeless, but the Grishams stood out on their balcony and helped over 200 people have a place to stay. Miraculously their home remained untouched by the hurricane exception of water in the basement. After all of these years and eleven hurricanes the house has only had one broken window. When Mr. Grisham died his wife sold the house to the catholic diocese and the bishop moved into the house. That's where the name comes from The Bishop's Palace."

"Wow," we all said in unison. After we bought our tickets, the gang walked closely together.

"Remember to look for the star because something is going to heat up," Andrea reminded us. Sure enough our tour guide, Mike pointed out a carved star above a still-working fireplace. I distracted Mike by asking several questions. The rest of the people on the tour were paying more attention to me than to my amigos, so Neils stuck her head into the fireplace and found the clue. She looked closely at the map and there was the fireplace with the star above it, and another clue was written on the back of the clue. It said, "Josephine was a doll."

"What does that mean?" Alison questioned.

"I don't know but let's keep listening to the tour guide and maybe we will find out who Josephine was," Andrea added. Sure enough Mike led us upstairs to where the Grisham's children slept. Josephine's room was the first one that we came to.

"Do you're I'm really into education act," Neils piped. So I did. I began asking Mike and the rest of the tour all kinds of questions about the children. What was really funny is that I really wanted to know about this family. Mrs. Grisham was an artist and painted her children's faces on the faces of the angels that were displayed around the lovely palace. Neils snuck under the rope and saw a beautiful really old doll. She reached underneath the doll's petticoat and there was another clue to finding the treasure.

"Hurry read it," Andrea begged.

"Wow. It says to find the international room. Look for the third tile from the gold and then push the tile carefully out with your fingers," Neils read.

The international bathroom was called that because the room was actually made from pieces all over the world: Italy, France and many other countries. When the tour began to move, Neils stayed put. But this time she wasn't so lucky.

"You, come here," said Mike our guide.

You need to stay with the group," he scolded. "Yes Sir. I'm sorry I just get so intrigued with the history. Would you mind taking me to see the doll, please," Neils begged.

"Okay, I will show you. I do understand your need to explore this fascinating house," Mike grinned.

Alison ran back into the bathroom, pushed the tile out and there in front of her beautiful blue eyes was the treasure of Jean Lafitte.

"John Lafitte's Treasure"

After the tour Nan and Pop went into the gift store. We were all jumping up and down and looking at all of the gold pieces and there were many that had been left in a small wooden chest with the words, "For the People".

"Are we the people?" Neils asked hopefully.

"No, but I believe our mysterious caller is," I said and then the cell phone rang.

"Hello," I whispered.

"You found it, didn't you?" the kid whispered back.

"Yes," I said. "What do we do now?"

"Meet me at Murdoch's Souvenir Shop on the seawall tonight at 7:00. You can give it to me then. And thank you so much." The kid then hung up.

"How are we going to know who it is," Alison asked. "I don't know," Andrea said, "But I have a feeling that we will just know."

"Mystery Solved"

After what seemed a lifetime we finally were able to go to Murdoch's and look for our mystery caller. I was on the other side of the shop with Neils when I heard,

"Hello Abby." I then heard Neils say,

"Hello Campbell. How are you and what are you doing here?" As Neils was asking this question, I already knew the answer.

"You are the mystery caller, aren't you Campbell?" I asked.

"Yes. It's me. Abby when I met all of you and you all told me about how you love to solve mysteries I knew that I could trust your gang. Since I'm in a wheelchair and my grandmother is so old, I needed help. You laughed and told me that day at the water park that your grandfather was your eyes. I thought that you could be my legs and help me to find the treasure. The treasure really belongs to my grandmother's family. You see, Abby and Neil, Jean Lafitte is our ancestor. My great grandfather was supposed to inherit the gold pieces but lawyers from everywhere began fighting over the treasure map, so he hid it.

My grandmother was cleaning out the attic when she stumbled upon the clues for the gold. I don't care so much about being rich, but it would be helpful for my grandmother to pay our bills." I leaned down and hugged Campbell and so did Neils.

"Meet us outside, Campbell," Neils commanded. "Alison has the gold pieces in her back pack. We'll hand them to you outside."

After the transaction took place, Neils and Andrea met all of us back upstairs in the shop. The four musketeers walked arm-in-arm with Nan and Pop following behind declaring that we would solve mysteries and make a difference in other people's lives for the rest of ours.

"À bientôt, À tout à l'heure" (*See you soon*)- Abby

Adventures of
Abby Diamond
(F 'abby'lous Activities)

Abby Diamond is a girl of mystery. She loves to solve the mysteries that are constantly surrounding her and her three best friends: Neils, Andrea, and Alison. Have fun doing the following activities after you read the novel. I have divided the activities into two sections:

Section One- Questions and activities from the novel.
Section Two- **"Braille is Fun"**- Learn about Braille and people who have a visual impairment.

Section One- "Abby Diamond Activities"

*In the section, "Out of Sight", Abby finds notes that are written in Braille. Go to the following website and copy the Braille alphabet, www.braillebug.org

*After reading over the Braille letters, write the following words in Braille: fun, Abby, friend

*In, "Out of Sight", the mystery note writer takes the kids on a scavenger hunt with the notes written in Braille since Abby is the only one in the group who can read Braille, she decodes the messages for everyone.
    Have fun with a group of friends by doing the following ABC Scavenger Hunt. Break

everyone into two groups. Every group gets a sheet with a list of every letter in the alphabet and a plastic baggy.

Go to a park and see what you can find for every letter of the alphabet. For example for letter "a", you may find an acorn. You will place the acorn in the baggy. If the object is too big for the baggy, break off a piece of it and place it in the baggy.

*Abby's family moves into their dream house. Make your dream house model home from a shoebox. Decorate it with colorful paper and small objects. Compare your dream house to a friend.

*Describe the major characters using one sentence per character on a large sheet of Manila paper. Cut out pictures from a magazine that remind you of each character. Label each picture with the character's name.

*Congratulations Katy! In the section, "Out of Sight", Katy just graduated from high school. Plan a party for Katy. Make a menu and invitations for the event.

*Illustrate Abby's family tree. After labeling

and drawing Abby's family tree, research your family's history. Draw your family tree underneath Abby's.

Grandmother Elizabeth	Nan and Pop
Emma, Caroline, Blake	Jacob, Dana
Katy	Katy
Abby	Abby
Chip	Chip

*In, "Alison, the Fourth Musketeer", Alison lies or so the kids in her class believe. Give Alison advice on how to stop lying.

*Alison is becoming one of the fourth musketeers. Write a poem on on friendship and write the meaning of it below.

*Compare Alison to 'Alison in Wonderland'. What are their similarities/differences?

*Make the following recipe for friendship bread. Serve your friends. (Don't forget adult supervision)

Friendship Cake with Starter

Starter :

3/4 cup drained peach chunks

3/4 cup drained pineapple

6 maraschino cherries, halved

1 1/2 cups granulated sugar

1 (1/4-ounce) package active dry yeast

Combine ingredients and place in a large glass jar with a loose cover at room temperature.

Stir several times the first day, once a day thereafter for 14 days. The starter will have fermented enough to start Friendship Cake Mix.

Friendship Cake Mix:

1 1/2 cups Starter

2 1/2 cups granulated sugar

1 (32-ounce) can sliced peaches with juice

Place into a gallon jar. Stir once a day for 10 days. Keep covered and at room temperature.

On 10th day add:

2 1/2 cups granulated sugar

1 (32-ounce) can chunk pineapple with juice

Stir once a day for 10 days.

On 20th day add:

2 1/2 cups granulated sugar

1 (10-ounce) jar maraschino cherries
1 (32-ounce) can fruit cocktail with juice
Stir once a day for 10 days.

On 30th day:

Drain juice from fruit. Divide juice into 5
    or 6 jars of 1 1/2 cups juice each and
    give to friend(s).
Divide the fruit into 3 equal parts. You will
    have enough to make 3 cakes.

Friendship Cake Mix Recipe:

1 (18.25-ounce) package yellow cake mix
(not pudding cake)
2/3 cup vegetable oil
4 large eggs
1 (4-ounce) package instant vanilla pudding
1 cup chopped nuts if you like
1/3 of the fruit (2 cups)
Combine with an electric mixer all
    ingredients and bake in greased and
    floured tube or Bundt pan at 350*F
    (175*C) for 50 to 60 minutes or until
    wooden pick inserted in center comes
    out clean.
Cool on wire rack in pan 15 minutes before
    removing.

*In, "Double Trouble", Abby is in a conflict with her look-alike cousin, Brooklyn. The two girls cannot get along until a fun afternoon of a large bubble that entangles the two. Have a bubble- chewing contest with some of your friends. Measure and see who can blow the largest and then the smallest bubble.

* What does the saying, "All that Glitters is not gold" mean to you? Make a list of other sayings and write down what they mean to you.

*Spray paint gold glitter on a few rocks. Hide the rocks and have your friends go on a treasure hunt just like Abby and her friends.

*Abby and her friends love the beach. Plan an indoor beach party. Place towels on the floor, add sand and seashells to buckets, etc. Add friends and your imagination.

*Buy several colors of yarn. Cut the pieces to fit around your and your friends' wrist. Twist the colors together and then make your friendship knots.

*Research Galveston, Texas. Plan a make-believe trip to the island.

*Research types of sea life that are becoming extinct. What can you do to help with this issue?

*Make a travel brochure for a dream vacation. Include: hotel, restaurants, places to visit and other exciting features of your vacation spot.

*Grandmother Elizabeth and Grand Pop and Nan are such wonderful grandparents to Abby. Do you have grandparents, aunts, uncles or extended family members who make your life better? Write them a thank you note and tell them why they mean so much to you and how much you appreciate them.

*Jean Lafitte was a pirate. What do you know about pirates? Write a paragraph about pirates. Make your own eye patch and sword from construction paper. Be creative.

*A Haiku poem originates from Japan. It consists of three lines: the first line has seven syllables, the second line has five and the last line has seven syllables. Write a Haiku poem for your best friend. Frame a picture of the two of you together, and give them their personal poem.

Section Two- Learning How to Read Braille

*Braille is fun to learn. Once you learn to decipher the code, you can be like Abby and learn to read Braille.

Are you ready to begin learning a new code? Clear your mind and get ready to look over the letters of the alphabet in Braille. (Look at the end of this chapter for a copy of the Braille alphabet letters)

First I want to give you a brief background on how Braille came to be.

Louis Braille was a brilliant fifteen year old student who was trying to read letters, numbers, etc. by using large tactual shapes since he was totally blinded after an accident when he was younger. He became frustrated when trying to read and write using large tactual letters, so Louis created a code (similar to Morris code). Louis was extremely intelligent so he composed a new code using the combination of six dots (dots 1-6) Go to www.afb.org and see and copy a picture of the Braille cell for the following activities.

There are two forms of Braille: uncontracted and contracted Braille or also known as grade 1 and grade 2 Braille. Do not get confused by the term grade. It does not have anything to do with grade levels: first and second grade. Grade one is the easier and uncontracted form of Braille. For example, none of the words are shortened simply spelled out like they are in print. The word little in grade one (uncontracted) Braille would be written out l-i-t-t-l-e, but if you wrote the word little in grade two (contracted) Braille it would be written ll (two L's). Grade two is less bulky and quicker for the students to write but can be more complicated for younger students to learn. There are over two hundred and forty-four contractions for Braille that are written in grade two.

Can you imagine anything in print being done also in Braille but only using the combination of six dots? I told you Louis Braille was a genius.

Grade two is very similar to learning short hand, however, in this lesson we are only going to discuss grade one, (uncontracted) Braille.

Take a look at the Braille cell again.

Look at the six dots and their places in the Braille cell. Dot 1 is in the first row at the top. Dot 2 is in the first row in the middle and dot 3 is in the first row at the bottom. Dots 4, 5, and 6 do the same in the second column.

Letter a sits on dot 1. Look back at your Braille cell. Letter a will sit on the first row at the top of the Braille cell on the left side.

Letter b sits on dots 1 and 2. Look again at your Braille cell. Letter b is on the first row and sits on the top and in the middle on the left side of the Braille cell.

Letter c sits on dots 1 and 4.

*Revisit the really cool website offered by The American Federation for the Blind. (www.braillebug.org) The website will demonstrate how to write all of your letters in Braille. You will find many activities that teach in a fun way how to write and read in Braille.

*Read the biography cards on famous people who had a visual impairment. (Located at the end of this chapter)

*Read information about Louis Braille from your biography card. Write down ten facts about Louis Braille.

In one of your ten facts describe why Braille is named after Louis Braille.

(Writing Center, Reading Center)

*Using your Braille alphabet write the following words in printed Braille. Make your dots with dark pencil so that others can read the dots that you make. Words: Braille, fun, hello, Louis, your own name, your best friend's name

*Turn on the DVD player and watch ten

minutes of the movie, <u>The Miracle Worker</u>. Describe the first, second and third segment of the movie. What obstacles did you observe that someone with a visual impairment may have? Who are the main characters in the segment that you watch? How does each respond to the obstacles of a child with a visual impairment? Describe how the child responds to her impairment?

(Reading Center, Writing Center)

*Read the information provided about James Thurber on your biography card. In spite of Mr. Thurber's visual impairment he became an accomplished cartoonist.

Make your own cartoon strip using a sentence strip or piece of Manila paper. After you have written your comic, color the pictures and read it to a friend.

Now wearing a blindfold, create another comic strip, color the pictures and compare the two comics.

(Reading Center, Art Center)

*Watch a five-ten minute clip of the movie Ray. Record the main idea from the movie clip that you watched. Describe the characters in the clip. Now read your biography card

on Ray Charles. Tell about a struggle that Ray Charles experienced with being visually impaired.
(Writing Center, Reading Center)

* Galileo was a famous astronomer and a mathematician who had a visual impairment. (Read your biography card on Galileo) Write five math problems and then change papers with a partner. Work your problems out with a calculator.
(Math Center, Writing Center)

*John Pulitzer was a newspaper report and well-known publisher who also had a visual impairment due to a retinal detachment.
Create your own classroom newspaper. Don't forget to include the following: Class News, Weather, Current Events, Comics and Horoscopes.
(Writing Center, Art Center)

*Make a tactual American flag for President Roosevelt. Use Tulip paint or wikki sticks to make the strips. Add tactual stars for the flag.

*Pretend that you are running for president.

Make your own campaign buttons and slogans.

(Art Center, Writing Center)

*Read about the physical challenges that were faced by our 32nd president, Franklin D. Roosevelt. President Roosevelt became visually impaired along with other disabilities from polio. (Read more about President Roosevelt on your biography card)

Pretend you are the president of the United States who has a visual impairment. Make a list of new rules (10) that will help people who have a visual impairment.

(Writing Center, Reading Center, Research Center)

*Research information about James Grover Thurber from your biography card. Write down five facts from your resource and site where you found the information.

*James Thurber also wrote novels and children's books. Look for information on his most famous children's book, The 13 Clocks. Write a three-line summary of the book. Using Manila paper, write your own children's book about a topic of your choice.

(Reading Center, Writing Center, Research Center)

*Harriet Tubman ran The Underground Railroad with a visual impairment. Read about Ms. Tubman from your biography card and describe The Underground Railroad using five sentences. What was an abolitionist? Define in one sentence.

(Reading Center, Research Center, Writing Center)

* Make a diorama of Harriet Tubman and The Underground Railroad. Use a shoebox, construction paper and any items that will make your project creative.

(Art Center)

*Use poster board and route a passage for slaves escaping from the south to the north. Route the passage that you created by gluing pieces of yarn on the route. Put on a blind- fold and feel of the passage not using your vision.

(Art Center)

*Franklin Roosevelt said the following quote, "You have nothing to fear but fear itself". Write down what you believe the quote is

saying. Do you believe in this quote? Explain why you feel this way.
   (Writing Center)

*Homer was a poet who was also visually impaired. Write a Haiku poem about a member of your family. (Haiku- originally from Japan- first line-5 syllables, second line- 7 syllables, third line-5 syllables)
   (Writing Center)

*Being healthy can improve your eyesight better. Make a five -day healthy diet. Illustrate a healthy diet that can improve someone's eye sight.
   (Writing Center, Art Center)

*Wear a blindfold and feel of all types of coins in a plastic baggy. Touch the outer edges of the coin and see if you can identify each coin correctly. Make a stack of each coin currency.
   (Math Center)

*Paint with sand- sprinkle sand in the paint, let dry. The next day feel of your artwork under blindfold.
   (Art Center)

*Research the parts of the eye. Illustrate the eye and label the following major parts: Iris, lens, pupil, optic nerve, sclera, retina and vitreous humor.
  (Research Center, Art Center)

*Feel of ten objects that have placed in a "feely" box while wearing a blindfold. List all ten objects on paper. How many do you answer correctly?
  (Writing Center)

*Listen to a recording of five dictation sentences. Try to write the sentences after listening to the tape once.

*Go to the American Federation for the Blind website (www.afb.org) and look for Braille Bug. Braille Bug teaches sighted children how to read the Braille alphabet with games, riddles and more fun.
  (Research Center)

*The word "eye" is called a palindrome. A palindrome means the word is spelled the same forward and backward. Write down as many palindromes as you can within five minutes. Race your partner.
  (Writing Center)

*In the lesson you learned that a baby who has a visual impairment must be taught to play. Brainstorm in your journal and write down at least 10 play activities that will encourage a baby with a visual impairment to move.
   (Writing Center, Research Center)

*Design a toy in your journal that would appeal to an infant who has a visual impairment. Name the toy and illustrate.
   (Art Center, Writing Center)

* Put on a blindfold and walk around the classroom. Use your hands to feel and to protect you from bumping into someone or something. Walk back to the center and write down your observations.
   (Writing Center)

*Make edible Play-doh under blindfold. Simply mix a white cake mix with peanut butter. You will want the same consistency as bread. Knead the dough and add food coloring for colors.
   Make a tactual recipe card for someone who cannot see. Be creative!
   (Writing Center, Reading Center)

*Study the list of alphabet whole words. Alphabet whole words are short forms of words to help make Braille easier to read and write. Every letter stands for a word such as, if you Braille a b it stands for but, a c stands for can, and a d stands for do. If I brailled an I a C and a G, in Braille it would read, "I can go". Below is a list of the fun alphabet whole words:

a- a, b-but, c-can, d-do, e-every, f-from, g-go, h-have, i-I, j-just, k-knowledge, l-like, m-more, n-not, o-o, p-people, q-quite, r-rather, s-so, t-that, u-us, v-very, w-will, x-it, y-you, z-as.

After saying the alphabet whole words write your own sentences using the short forms. I'll get you started. 1) I L Y= I like you. Isn't that fun? Do the rest on your own.

(Reading Center, Writing Center)

*People who have a visual impairment must learn to fold money correctly so that they can feel into their billfold and know which bill is what. Use play money, put on your blindfold, and fold the money in a unique way that tells you what each bill is worth. Write a money word problem for a partner.

(Math Center, Writing Center)

*Claude Monet was a brilliant artist who lost his vision. Researchers who studied his paintings noticed deficits in his work due to his loss of vision. (Read your biography card on Monet)

Take pieces of colorful tissue paper and create your own motif by gluing the pieces on a large sheet of Manila paper.
(Reading Center, Art Center)

* Claude Monet also made beautiful paintings of water lilies and loved the ocean. Illustrate one of the above using bright and vivid colors.

*Take a small piece of rubber and a pin. Make a tactual picture by pushing the pin in and out of the rubber.
(Art Center)

*Research how to find materials for the blind and visually impaired. Write down all of your sources.
(Writing Center, Research Center)

*Squeeze inexpensive gel into a zip-lock baggy. Place small items into the gel carefully placing them apart from one another. Ask a partner to wear a blindfold and to fill what

is inside of the gel bag. Ask him to write down everything that he believes he felt.
   (Art Center, Writing Center)

*Read the following poem written by Jamille Smith. Try to memorize as much of the poem as you can within five minutes. In your journal, summarize the poem and illustrate what is happening throughout the poem. Write three words using the Braille alphabet.
   (Reading Center, Writing Center)

Yasmine Learns Braille
BY: Jamille Smith
One, two, three, four;

Three, two and one.

Reading Braille is hard,

But it's getting to be fun!

The letter "c" is can,

And "g" means go.

There are many more letters

That I really need to know

What is "X"? I asked.

I found out that it is "It".

All of the letters in Braille

Have a word that will fit.

"From" is just the letter "f"

And "Y" is the word "You"

P is the sign for people

And D is what they "do".

When you've learned every letter,

You are still not done.

Three, four, five, six "a"

Stands for number "1".

I know it sounds confusing,

And it really can be.

But reading words in Braille

Is making sense to me

Claude Monet

Claude Monet was a brilliant and talented artist. Monet's paintings were painted in different types of motifs. He especially loved to paint water lilies and the ocean. Because of retinal problems he began to lose his sight.

Monet had to memorize the colors on his pallet, so that he could continue to paint. However, researchers were able to see differences in his paintings after he began to lose his sight.

Joseph Pulitzer

Joseph Pulitzer was a great newspaperman, publisher and reporter.

He turned sales of newspapers that were going bankrupt into big sellers by adding Human Interest stories, scandals and interesting topics to people.

There is a prestigious award named after Pulitzer given to award-winning authors.

Pulitzer began to lose his vision from retinal problems and had to retire from the business.

President Franklin Roosevelt

President Franklin Roosevelt was the 32nd president of the United States during the Great Depression and World War II. He was given credit for restoring the country back from poverty and hopelessness. For his strong leadership ability, he was elected into office of president of the United States for four terms longer than any other president.

President Roosevelt was physically impaired as well as visually impaired from a case of polio.

Helen Keller

Helen Adams Keller was born perfectly

normal until a high fever left her deaf and blind at the age of 19 months. However, after a very strong-willed and skilled teacher named Ann Sullivan taught her sign language and Braille, Helen became known as a world famous speaker, author and advocate for the disabled.

Louis Braille

Louis Braille became blind as a young boy when he struck himself in the eye with one of his father's tools. The infection spread to the other eye, so Louis was totally blind.

Back in the 1800's people who were blind attempted to read large tactual letters and numbers which was difficult, slow and frustrating.

Louis was very intelligent and devised a code similar to Morris code from the combination of six dots. He reasoned that persons with a visual impairment would be able to read and write at a comparable speed of sighted readers if they would learn to read and write the Braille code.

Galileo Galilei

Galileo Galileu was a brilliant astronomer, mathematician and physicist. Galilei was the first person to discover Jupiter and its moons. Since he discovered the moons they have been named in his honor.

Galilei became totally blind by the age of 68.

John Milton

John Milton was a poet and author most remembered by his epic poem, "Paradise Lost". Milton was born in the 1600's and was very outspoken about religion and politics.

He did not fit in with others during his boyhood because of his radical views.

Milton was bitter when he became visually impaired and wrote about the struggles of having a visual impairment.

Homer

Homer lived during the dark Greek ages. Little is known about him other than his brilliant writing The Odyssey.

Homer was blind and would often tell Shakespearian tales to others.

Harriet Tubman

Harriet Tubman was a slave during the Civil War times. She and others who were slaves were treated like animals, so she escaped to

Canada. Tubman experienced vision loss and seizures after she was savagely hit in the head by a slave owner.

Harriet did not stay in Canada, however. She began helping other slaves escape up north by what was called an Underground Railroad. The Underground Railroad were houses where slaves could stay until their next journey closer to the north.

Ray Charles

Ray Charles lived during the 1930 until 2004. He was a wonderful jazz and blues singer, composer and entertainer. While Ray struggled with problems he became a musical legend and won many Grammy's and other awards. Ray also wrote music and songs in Braille for many large bands. Later on in his life, Ray sang, "We Are the World", with many other famous entertainers in order to end hunger in Africa.

Stevie Wonder

Stevie Wonder was born in 1950. He has sold many records, CD's and songs.

Wonder has won multiple Grammy awards and has been inducted into the Music Hall of Fame.

Stevie Wonder does not only sing but can play multiple instruments.

In conclusion of section two, I hope that you have had fun while learning about others who have a visual impairment as well as being able to read the first steps in Braille.

It is my belief that we are all disabled in some way; some ways are just not as visible as someone who cannot see.

I love the quote from a former Mousekeeter:

"Life does not have to be perfect to be wonderful." -- Annette Funicello